"'LOOK! LOOK! THERE BY THOSE LITTLE BUSHES!'"

Santa Fé's Partner

Being Some Memorials of Events in a
New-Mexican Track-end Town

By

Thomas A. Janvier

Author of
"The Passing of Thomas" "The Uncle of an Angel"
"The Aztec Treasure - House"
"In the Sargasso Sea"
Etc. Etc.

New York and London
Harper & Brothers Publishers
1907

TO

C. A. J.

Contents

CHAP.   PAGE

I.   PALOMITAS   1

II.   THE SAGE-BRUSH HEN 15

III. HART'S NEPHEW'S HOLD-UP 44

IV. SANTA FÉ CHARLEY'S KINDERGARTEN . . 77

V.   BOSTON'S LION-HUNT 127

VI. SHORTY SMITH'S HANGING 163

VII. THE PURIFICATION OF PALOMITAS . . . 208

Illustrations

"'LOOK! LOOK! THERE BY THOSE LITTLE BUSHES!'" . . . . *Frontispiece*

"HER LEFT HAND WAS LAYING IN HER LAP, AND THE OLD GENT GOT A-HOLD OF IT" *Facing p.* 22

"WROTE OUT A NOTICE THAT WAS TACKED UPON THE DEEPO DOOR" . . . . . " 84

"'ONE OF THE NEW GERMAN KINDERGARTEN APPLIANCES'" . . . . " 120

"STARING 'ROUND THE PLACE SAME AS IF HE'D STRUCK A MENAGERIE" . . . " 132

"'IT'S HOTTER THAN SAHARA!' SAID THE ENGLISHMAN" . . . . " 166

"AND DOWN HART WENT IN A HEAP ON THE FLOOR" . . . . " 196

"'DON'T HANG HIM, SIR!' SHE GROANED OUT" . . . . " 224

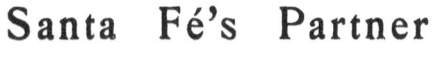

Santa Fé's Partner

Santa Fé's Partner

I

PALOMITAS

'VE been around considerable in the Western Country—mostly some years back—and I've seen quite a little, one way and another, of the folks living there: but I can't really and truly say I've often come up with them nature's noblemen — all the time at it doing stunts in natural nobility — the story-books make out is the chief population of them parts. Like enough the young fellers from the East who write such sorts of books — having plenty of spare time for writing, while they're giving their feet a rest to get

the ache out—do come across 'em, same as they say they do; but I reckon the herd's a small one—and, for a fact, if you could cross the book brand with the kind you mostly meet on the ranges the breed would be improved.

Cow-punchers and prospectors and such don't look like and don't act like what tenderfoots is accustomed to, and so they size 'em up to be different all the way through. They ain't. They're just plain human nature, same as the rest of us — only more so, through not being herded close in. About the size of it is, most folks needs barbed wire to keep 'em from straying. In a rough country—where laws and constables ain't met with frequent — a good-sized slice of the population 's apt to run wild. With them that's white, it don't much matter. The worst you can say against 'em is, they sometimes do a little more shooting than seems really needed; but such doings is apt to have a show of reason at the bottom of 'em, and don't happen often anyhow—most being satisfied to work off their high spirits some

Palomitas

other way. With them that's not white, things is different. When the Apache streak gets on top it sends 'em along quick into clear deviltry—the kind that makes you cussed just for the sake of cussedness and not caring a damn; and it's them that has give some parts of the Western Country—like it did New Mexico in the time I'm talking about, when they was bunched thick there—its bad name.

In the long run, of course, the toughs is got rid of—being shoved out or hung out, at first by committees and later on in regular shape by sheriffs and marshals—and things is quieted down. It's the everlasting truth, though, that them kind of mavericks mostly is a blame sight commoner in parts just opened than the story-book kind—that's always so calm-eyed and gentle-natured and generous and brave. What's more, I reckon they'll keep on being commoner, human nature not being a thing that changes much, till we get along to the Day of Judgment roundup—and the goats is cut out and corralled for keeps.

Santa Fé's Partner

For certain, it was goats was right up at the head of the procession in the Territory in my time—which was the time when the railroads was a-coming in—and in them days things was rough. The Greasers living there to start with wasn't what you might call sand-papered; and the kind of folks found in parts railroads has just got to, same as I've mentioned, don't set out to be extry smooth. Back East they talked about the higher civilization that was overflowing New Mexico; but, for a cold fact, the higher civilization that did its overflowing on that section mostly had a sheriff on its tracks right along up to the Missouri—and the rest of the way done what it blame felt like, and used a gun.

Some of them native Mexicans wasn't bad fighters. When they went to hacking at one another with knives—the way they was used to—they often done right well. But when they got up against the higher civilization—which wasn't usually less 'n half drunk, and went heeled with two Colt's and a Winchester—they found out they'd bit off more'n they

4

Palomitas

could chew. Being sandy, they kept at it—
but the civilizers was apt to have the call.
And in between times, when the two of 'em—
the Greasers and the civilizers—wasn't taking the change out of each other, they both
of 'em took it out of anybody who happened
to come along.

Yes, sirree!—in them days things was a
good deal at loose ends in the Territory.
When you went anywheres, if you was going
alone, you always felt you'd better leave
word what trail you took: that is, if you was
fussy in such matters, and wanted what the
coyotes left of you brought in by your
friends and planted stylish—with your name,
and when it happened, painted on a board.

This place where the track got stuck—
sticking partly because there was trouble
with the Atchison, and partly because the
Company couldn't for close onto a year jag
any more out of the English stockholders to
build on with—was up on a bluff right over
the Rio Grande and was called Palomitas.
Being only mostly Greasers and Indians liv-

5

ing in the Territory—leaving out the white folks at Santa Fé and the army posts, and the few Germans there was scattered about—them kind of queer-sounding names was what was mainly used.

It wasn't never meant to be no sort of an American town nohow, Palomitas wasn't—being made to start with of 'dobes (which is Mexican for houses built of mud, and mud they was in the rainy season) spilled around on the bluff anywheres; and when the track come along through the middle of it the chinks was filled in with tents and shingle-shacks and dugouts—all being so mixed up and scattery you'd a-thought somebody'd been packing a town through them parts in a wagon and the load had jolted out, sort of casual over the tail-board, and stuck where it happened to come down. The only things you could call houses was the deepo, and the Forest Queen Hotel right across the track from it, and Bill Hart's store. Them three buildings was framed up respectable; with real windows that opened, and doors such as you could move without kicking at 'em till

6

Palomitas

you was tired. The deepo was right down stylish—having a brick chimney and being painted brown. Aside the deepo was the tank and the windmill that pumped into it. Seems to me at nights, sometimes, I can hear that old windmill going around creaking and clumpetty-clumpetting now!

Palomitas means "little doves"—but I reckon the number of them birds about the place was few. For about a thousand years, more or less, it had been run on a basis of two or three hundred Mexicans and a sprinkling of pigs and Pueblo Indians—the pigs was the most respectable—and it was allowed to be, after the track got there, the toughest town the Territory had to show. Santa Cruz de la Cañada, which was close to it, was said to have took the cake for toughness before railroad times. It was a holy terror, Santa Cruz was! The only decent folks in it was the French padre — who outclassed most saints, and hadn't a fly on him—and a German named Becker. He had the Government forage-station, Becker had; and he used to say he'd had a fresh surprise every

7

Santa Fé's Partner

one of the mornings of the five years he'd
been forage-agent—when he woke up and
found nobody'd knifed him in the night and
he was keeping on being alive!

But when the track come in, and the
higher civilization come in a-yelling with it
and spread itself, Palomitas could give points
to the Cañada in cussedness all down the
line. Most of it right away was saloons and
dance-halls; and the pressure for faro accom-
modation was such the padre thought he
could make money by closing down his own
monte-bank and renting. Denver Jones took
his place at fifty dollars a week, payable every
Saturday night—and rounded on the padre
by getting back his rent-money over the table
every Sunday afternoon. He'd a-got it back
Sunday mornings if the padre hadn't been
tied up mornings to his work. (He was a
native, that padre was — and went on so
extra outrageous his own folks couldn't stand
him and Bishop Lamy bounced him from his
job.) Pretty much all the time there was
rumpusses; and the way they was managed
made the Mexicans—being used, same as I've

Palomitas

said, to knives mostly—open their eyes wide.
It seemed really to jolt 'em when they begun
to find out what a live man with his back
up could do with a gun! Occurrences was
so frequent—before construction started up
again, and for a while after—the new cemetery out in the sage-brush on the mesa
come close to having as big a population as
the town.

What happened—shootings, and doings of
all sorts — mostly centred on the Forest
Queen. That was the only place that called
itself a hotel in Palomitas—folks being able
to get some sort of victuals there, and it having bunks in a room off the bar-room where
passers-through was give a chance to think
(by morning they was apt to think different)
they was going to have a night's sleep.
Kicking against what you got—and against
the throwed-in extras you'd a-been better
without—didn't do no good. Old Tenderfoot
Sal, who kept the place, only stuck her fat
elbows out and told the kickers she done the
best she knowed how to, and she reckoned it
was as good as you could expect in them

parts, and most was suited. If they didn't
like the Forest Queen Hotel, she said, they
was free to get out of it and go to one that
suited 'em better—and as there wasn't none
to go to, Sal held the cards.

She was a corker, Sal was! By her own
account of herself, she'd learned hotel-keep-
ing through being a sutler's wife in the war.
What sutling had had to do with it was left
to guess at, and there was opinions as to how
much her training in hoteling had done for
her; but it was allowed she'd learned a heap
of other things—of one sort and another—
and her name of Tenderfoot was give her
because them fat feet of hers, in the course
of her travels, had got that hard I reckon
she wouldn't a-noticed it walking on red-hot
point-upwards ten-penny nails!

In the Forest Queen bar-room was the biggest bank there was in town. Blister Mike—
he was Irish, Blister was, and Sal's bar-keep
—had some sort of a share in it; but it was
run by a feller who'd got the name of Santa
Fé Charley, he having had a bank over in
Santa Fé afore Sal give him the offer to come

Palomitas

across to Palomitas and take charge. He
was one of the blue-eyed quiet kind, Charley
was, that's not wholesome to monkey with;
the sort that's extra particular about being
polite and nice-spoken—and never makes no
mistakes, when shooting-time comes, about
shooting to kill. When he was sober, though
—and he had to keep sober, mostly, or his
business would a-suffered—he wasn't hunting after rumpusses: all he did was to keep
ready for 'em, and hold his end up when they
come along. He had the habit—same as
some other of the best card sharps I've met
with—of dressing himself in black, real stylish: wearing a long-tail coat and a boiled
shirt and white tie, and having a toney wide-
brimmed black felt hat that touched him off
fine. With them regular fire-escape clothes
on, folks was apt to take him for one; and,
when they did, he always met 'em half-way
by letting on preaching was his business—
till he got 'em on the other side of the table
and begun to shake down what cards he
needed from up inside them black coat-
sleeves. Mostly they ended by thinking that

maybe preaching wasn't just what you might call his strongest hold.

It helped him in his work more'n a little, sometimes, dressing up that way and talking to suit, like he knowed how to, real high-toned talk; but I do believe for a fact he enjoyed the dollars he got out of it less 'n he did the fun it give him making fools of folks by setting up rigs on 'em — he truly being the greatest hand at rigging I ever seen. Somehow—not having the comfort of being able to get drunk half as often as he wanted to—it seemed like he give himself the let-out he needed in them queer antics; and, for certain, he managed 'em always so they went with a hum. When him and the Sage-Brush Hen played partners in rigging anybody—as they was apt to, the Hen being much such another and so special friends with Charley she'd come on after him from Santa Fé— there mostly was a real down spirited game!

She was what you might call the leading lady in the Forest Queen dance-hall, the Sage - Brush Hen was; and if you wanted fun, and had to choose between her and a

Palomitas

basket of monkeys, all I've got to say is—
nobody'd ever a-took the monkeys who
knowed the Hen! That girl was up to
more queer tricks than anybody of her size
and shape—she had a powerful fine shape,
the Hen had—I've ever laid eyes on; and
she'd run 'em in you so slick and quiet—
keeping as demure as a cat after birds while
she was doing it—you'd never suspicion anything was happening till you found the whole
town laughing its head off at you for being
so many kinds of a fool!

Things wasn't any time what you might
call too extra quiet in Palomitas; but when
them two—the Hen and Santa Fé—started
in together to run any racket you may bet
your life there was a first-class circus from
the word go! Grass didn't grow much under
their feet, either. The very minute the Hen
struck the town—coming on after Santa Fé,
same as I've said, and him waiting for her
when she got there—they went at their mon-
key-shining, finishing two-handed what the
Hen had started as a lone-hand game. Right
along from then on they kept things moving

13

spirited, one way and another, without much
of a let-up. And they ended off—the day
the two of 'em, owing to circumstances, lit
out together—by setting up on all of us what
I reckon was the best rig ever set up on anybody anywheres since rigs was begun!

Palomitas was a purer town, Cherry said—
it was him led off in the purifying—after we
was shut of 'em, and of some others that was
fired for company; and I won't say he wasn't
right in making out it was a better town,
maybe, when we'd got it so blame pure.
But they had their good points, the Hen and
Santa Fé had—and after they was purified
out of it some of us didn't never quite feel
as if the place was just the same.

II

THE SAGE-BRUSH HEN

THE Hen blew in one day on Hill's coach, coming from Santa Fé, setting up on the box with him—Hill run his coach all the time the track was stuck at Palomitas, it being quicker for Santa Fé folks going up that way to Pueblo and Denver and Leadville than taking the Atchison out to El Moro and changing to the Narrow Gauge—and she was so all over dust that Wood sung out to him: "Where'd you get your Sage-Brush Hen from?" And the name stuck.

More folks in Palomitas had names that had tumbled to 'em like that than the kind that had come regular. And even when they sounded regular they likely wasn't. Regular

Santa Fé's Partner

names pretty often got lost coming across the
Plains in them days—more'n a few finding it
better, about as they got to the Missouri, to
leave behind what they'd been called by back
East and draw something new from the pack.
Making some sort of a change was apt to be
wholesomer and often saved talk.

Hill said the Hen was more fun coming
across from Santa Fé than anything he'd
ever got up against; and she was all the
funnier, he said, because when he picked her
up at the Fonda she looked like as if butter
wouldn't melt in her mouth and started in
with her monkey-shines so sort of quiet and
demure. Along with her, waiting at the
Fonda, was an old gent with spectacles who
turned out to be a mine sharp—one of them
fellows the Government sends out to the
Territory to write up serious in books all the
fool stories prospectors and such unload on
'em: the kind that needs to be led, and 'll
eat out of your hand. The Hen and the old
gent and Hill had the box-seat, the Hen in
between; and she was that particular about
her skirts climbing up, and about making

16

room after she got there, that Hill said he
sized her up himself for an officer's wife going
East.

Except to say thank you, and talk polite
that way, she didn't open her head till they'd
got clear of the town and begun to go slow
in that first bit of bad road among the sand-
hills; and it was the old gent speaking to her
—telling her it was a fine day, and he hoped
she liked it—that set her stamps to working
a little then. She allowed the weather was
about what it ought to be, and said she was
much obliged and it suited her; and then she
got her tongue in behind her teeth again as
·if she meant to keep it there—till the old
gent took a fresh start by asking her if she'd
been in the Territory long. She said polite
she hadn't, and was quiet for a minute.
Then she got out her pocket-handkerchief
and put it up to her eyes and said she'd
been in it longer'n she wanted, and was
glad she was going away. Hill said her
talking that way made him feel kind of
curious himself; but he didn't have no need
to ask questions—the old gent saving him

that trouble by going for her sort of fatherly and pumping away at her till he got the whole thing.

It come out scrappy, like as might be expected, Hill said; and so natural-sounding he thought he must be asleep and dreaming— he knowing pretty well what was going on in the Territory, and she telling about doings that was news to him and the kind he'd a-been sure to hear a lot of if they'd ever really come off. Hill said he wished he could tell it all as she did—speaking low,. and ketching her breath in the worst parts, and mopping at her eyes with her pocket-handkerchief —but he couldn't; and all he could say about it was it was better'n any theatre show he'd ever seen. The nubs of it was, he said, that she said her husband had taken out a troop from Fort Wingate against the Apaches (Hill knew blame well up there in the Navajo country was no place to look for Apaches) and the troop had been ambushed in a cañon in the Zuñi Mountains (which made the story still tougher) and every man of 'em, along with her "dear Captain" as she

The Sage-Brush Hen

called him, had lost his hair. "His loved remains are where those fierce creatures left them," she said. "I have not even the sad solace of properly burying his precious bones!" And she cried.

The old gent was quite broke up, Hill said, and took a-hold of her hand fatherly—she was a powerful fine-looking woman—and said she had his sympathy; and when she eased up on her crying so she could talk she said she was much obliged—and felt it all the more, she said, because he looked like a young uncle of hers who'd brought her up, her father being dead, till she was married East to her dear Captain and had come out to the Territory with him to his dreadful doom.

Hill said it all went so smooth he took it down himself at first—but he got his wind while she was crying, and he asked her what her Captain's name was, and what was his regiment; telling her he hadn't heard of any trouble up around Wingate, and it was news to him Apaches was in them parts. She give him a dig in the ribs with her elbow —as much as to tell him he wasn't to ask no such questions—and said back to him her dear husband was Captain Chiswick of the Twelfth Cavalry; and it had been a big come down for him, she said, when he got his commission in the Regulars, after he'd been a Volunteer brigadier-general in the war.

Hill knowed right enough there wasn't no Twelfth Cavalry nowhere, and that the boys at Wingate was A and F troops of the Fourth; but he ketched on to the way she was giving it to the old gent—and so *he* give *her* a dig in the ribs, and said he'd knowed Captain Chiswick intimate, and he was as good a fellow as ever was, and it was a blame pity he was killed. She give him a dig back again, at that—and was less particular about making room on his side.

The old gent took it all in, just as it come along; and after she'd finished up about the Apaches killing her dear Captain he wanted to know where she was heading for—because if she was going home East, he said, he was going East himself and could give her a father's care.

The Sage-Brush Hen

She said back to him, pleasant like, that a young man like him couldn't well be fathering an old lady like her, though it was obliging of him to offer; but, anyway, she wasn't going straight back East, because she had to wait awhile at Palomitas for a remittance she was expecting to pay her way through— and she wasn't any too sure about it, she said, whether she'd get her remittance; or, if she did get it, when it would come. Everything bad always got down on you at once, she said; and just as the cruel savages had slain her dear Captain along come the news the bank East he'd put his money in had broke the worst kind. Her financial difficulties wasn't a patch on the trouble her sorrowing heart was giving her, she said; but she allowed they added what she called pangs of bitterness to her deeper pain.

The old gent—he wasn't a fool clean through—asked her what was the matter with her Government transportation; she having a right to transportation, being an officer's widow going home. Hill said he give her a nudge at that, as much as to

Santa Fé's Partner

say the old gent had her. She didn't faze
a bit, though. It was her Government
transportation she was waiting for, she
cracked back to him smooth and natural;
but such things had to go all the way to
Washington to be settled, she said, and
then come West again—Hill said he 'most
snickered out at that—and she'd known
cases when red-tape had got in the way and
transportation hadn't been allowed at all.
Then she sighed terrible, and said it might
be a long, long while before she could get
home again to her little boy—who was all
there was left her in the world. Her little
Willy was being took care of by his grand-
mother, she said, and he was just his father's
own handsome self over again—and she got
out her pocket-handkerchief and jammed it
up to her eyes.

Her left hand was laying in her lap, sort of
casual, and the old gent got a-hold of it and
said he didn't know how to tell her how sorry
he was for her. Talking from behind her
pocket-handkerchief, she said such sympathy
was precious; and then she went on, kind of

[See p. 22

"HER LEFT HAND WAS LAYING IN HER LAP, AND THE OLD GENT
GOT A-HOLD OF IT"

The Sage-Brush Hen

pitiful, saying she s'posed her little Willy'd
have forgot all about her before she'd get
back to him—and she cried some more. Hill
said she done it so well he was half took in
himself for a minute, and felt so bad he went
to licking and swearing at his mules.

After a while she took a brace—getting
down her pocket-handkerchief, and calling
in the hand the old gent was a-holding—and
said she must be brave, like her dear Captain 'd always been, so he'd see when he
was a-looking at her from heaven she was
doing the square thing. And as to having
to wait around before she went East, she
said, in one way it didn't make any matter—
seeing she'd be well cared for and comfortable
at Palomitas staying in the house of the
Baptist minister, who'd married her aunt.

Hill said when she went to talking about
Baptist ministers and aunts in Palomitas he
shook so laughing inside he most fell off the
box. Except the Mexican padre who belonged there—the one I've spoke of that
made a record, and Bishop Lamy had to
bounce—and sometimes the French ones

from San Juan and the Cañada, who was
straight as strings, there wasn't a fire-escape
ever showed himself in Palomitas; and as
to the ladies of the town—well, the ladies
wasn't just what you'd call the aunt kind.
It's a cold fact that Palomitas, that year
when the end of the track stuck there, was
the cussedest town, same as I've said it was,
in the whole Territory — and so it was no
more'n natural Hill should pretty near bust
himself trying to hold in his laughing when
the Hen took to talking so off-hand about
Palomitas and Baptist ministers and aunts.
She felt how he was shaking, and jammed
him hard with her elbow to keep him
from letting his laugh out and giving her
away.

Hill said they'd got along to Pojuaque by
the time the Hen had finished telling about
herself, and the fix she was in because she
had to wait along with her aunt in Palomitas
till her transportation come from Washington
—and she just sick to get East and grab her
little Willy in her arms. And the old gent

The Sage-Brush Hen

was that interested in it all, Hill said, it was
a sight to see how he went on.

At Pojuaque the coach always made a
noon stop, and the team was changed and
the passengers got dinner at old man Bouquet's. He was a Frenchman, old man
Bouquet was; but he'd been in the Territory
from 'way back, and he'd got a nice garden
behind his house and things fixed up French
style. His strongest hold was his wine-mak-
ing. He made a first-class drink, as drinks
of that sort go; and, for its kind, it was
pretty strong. As his cooking was first-class
too, Hill's passengers—and the other folks
that stopped for grub there—always wanted
to make a good long halt.

Hill said it turned out the old gent knowed
how to talk French, and that made old man
Bouquet extra obliging — and he set up a
rattling good dinner and fetched out some of
the wine he said he was in the habit of keeping for his own drinking, seeing he'd got
somebody in the house for once who really
could tell the difference between good and
bad. He fixed up a table out in the garden

25

—aside of that queer tree, all growed together, he thought so much of — and set
down with 'em himself; and Hill said it was
one of the pleasantest parties he'd ever been
at in all his born days.

The Hen and the old gent got friendlier
and friendlier—she being more cheerful when
she'd been setting at table a while, and getting to talking so comical she kept 'em all
on a full laugh. Now and then, though,
she'd pull up sudden and kind of back away
—making out she didn't want it to show so
much—and get her pocket-handkerchief to
her eyes and snuffle; and then she'd pull
herself together sort of conspicuous, and say
she didn't want to spoil the party, but she
couldn't help thinking how long it was likely
to be before she'd see her little boy. And
then the old gent would say that such tender
motherliness did her credit, and hers was a
sweet nature, and he'd hold her hand till she
took it away.

Hill said the time passed so pleasant he
forgot how it was going, and when he happened to think to look at his watch he found

The Sage-Brush Hen

he'd have to everlastingly hustle his mules to get over to Palomitas in time to ketch the Denver train. He went off in a tearing hurry to hitch up, and old man Bouquet went along to help him—the old gent saying he guessed he and Mrs. Chiswick would stay setting where they was, it being cool and comfortable in the garden, till the team was put to. They set so solid, Hill said, they didn't hear him when he sung out to 'em he was ready; and he said he let his mouth go wide open and yelled like hell. (Hill always talked that careless way. He didn't mean no harm by it. He said it was just a habit he'd got into driving mules.) They not coming, he went to hurry 'em, he said—and as he come up behind 'em the Hen was stuffing something into her frock, and the old gent was saying: "I want you to get quickly to your dear infant, my daughter. You can return at your convenience my trifling loan. And now I will give you a fatherly kiss—"

But he didn't, Hill said—because the Hen heard Hill's boots on the gravel and faced round so quick she spoiled his chance. He seemed a little jolted, Hill said; but the Hen was so cool, and talked so pleasant and natural about what a nice dinner they'd been having, and what a fine afternoon it was, he braced up and got to talking easy too.

Then they all broke for the coach, and got away across the Tesuque River and on through the sand-hills — with Hill cutting away at his mules and using words to 'em fit to blister their hides off—and when they fetched the Cañada they'd about ketched up again to schedule time. After the Mexican who kept the Santa Cruz post-office had made the mess he always did with the mail matter, and had got the cussing he always got from Hill for doing it, they started off again—coming slow through that bit of extra heavy road along by the Rio Grande, but getting to the deepo at Palomitas all serene to ketch the Denver train.

All the way over from Pojuaque, Hill said, he could see out of the corner of his eye the old gent was nudging up to the Hen with his shoulder, friendly and sociable; and he said he noticed the Hen was a good deal less par-

The Sage-Brush Hen

ticular about making room. The old gent
flushed up and got into a regular temper,
Hill said, when Wood sung out as they
pulled in to the deepo platform: "Where'd
you get your Sage-Brush Hen from?"—and
that way give her what stuck fast for her
name.

As it turned out, they might a-kept on
a-hashing as long as they'd a mind to at
Pojuaque; and Hill might a-let his mules
take it easy, without tiring himself swearing
at 'em, on a dead walk—there being a wash-
out in the Comanche Cañon, up above the
Embudo, that held the train. It wasn't
much of a wash-out, the conductor said; but
he said he guessed all hands likely'd be more
comfortable waiting at Palomitas, where
there was things doing, than they would be
setting still in the cañon while the track-gang
finished their job—and he said he reckoned
the train wouldn't start for about three
hours.

The Hen and the old gent was standing
on the deepo platform, where they'd landed

from the coach; and Hill said as he was taking his mails across to the express-car he heard him asking her once more if she hadn't better come right along East to her lonely babe; and promising to take a father's care of her all the way. The Hen seemed to be in two minds about it for a minute, Hill said, and then she thanked him, sweet as sugar, for his goodness to her in her time of trouble; and told him it would be a real comfort to go East with such a kind escort to take care of her—but she said it wouldn't work, because she was expected in Palomitas, and not stopping there would be disappointing to her dear uncle and aunt.

It was after sundown and getting duskish, while they was talking; and she said she must be getting along. The old gent said he'd go with her; but she said he mustn't think of it, as it was only a step to the parsonage and she knew the way. While he was keeping on telling her she really must let him see her safe with her relatives, up come Santa Fé Charley—and Charley sung out: "Hello, old girl. So you've got here!

The Sage-Brush Hen

I was looking for you on the coach, and I thought you hadn't come."

Hill said he begun to shake all over with laughing; being sure—for all Charley in his black clothes and white tie looked so toney—it would be a dead give away for her. But he said she only give a little jump when Santa Fé sung out to her, and didn't turn a hair.

"Dear Uncle Charley, I *am* so glad to see you!" she said easy and pleasant; and then round she come to the old gent, and said as smooth as butter to him: "This is my uncle, the Baptist minister, sir, come to take me to the parsonage to my dear aunt. It's almost funny to have so young an uncle! Aunt's young too—you see, grandfather married a second time. We're more like sister and brother—being so near of an age; and he always will talk to me free and easy, like he always did—though I tell him now he's a minister it don't sound well." And then she whipped round to Charley, so quick he hadn't time to get a word in edgeways, and said to him: "I hope Aunt Jane's well, and didn't have to go up to Denver—as she said she might in her last letter—to look after Cousin Mary. And I do hope you've finished the painting she said was going on at the parsonage—so you can take me in there till my transportation comes and I can start East. This kind gentleman, who's going up on to-night's train, has been offering—and it's just as good of him, even if I can't go—to escort me home to my dear baby; and he's been giving me in the sweetest way his sympathy over my dear husband Captain Chiswick's loss."

Hill said he never knowed anybody take cards as quick as Santa Fé took the cards the Hen was giving him. "I'm very happy to meet you, sir," he said to the old gent; "and most grateful to you for your kindness to my poor niece Rachel in her distress. We have been sorrowing over her during Captain Chiswick's long and painful illness—"

"My dear Captain had been sick for three months, and got up out of his bed to go and be killed with his men by those dreadful Apaches," the Hen cut in.

The Sage-Brush Hen

" —and when the news came of the massacre," Charley went right on, as cool as an iced drink, "our hearts almost broke for her. Captain Chiswick was a splendid gentleman, sir; one of the finest officers ever sent out to this Territory. His loss is a bad thing for the service; but it is a worse thing for my poor niece — left forsaken along with her sweet babes. They are noble children, sir; worthy of their noble sire!"

"Oh, Uncle Charley!" said the Hen. "Didn't you get my letter telling you my little Jane died of croup? I've only my little Willy, now!" And she kind of gagged.

"My poor child: My poor child!" said Santa Fé. "I did not know that death had winged a double dart at you like that—your letter never came." And then he said to the old gent: "The mail service in this Territory, sir, is a disgrace to the country. The Government ought to be ashamed!"

Hill said while they was giving it and taking it that way he most choked—particular as the old gent just gulped it all down whole.

Hill said the three of 'em was sort of quiet

33

and sorrowful for a minute, and then Santa Fé said: "It is too bad, Rachel, but your Aunt Jane did have to go up to Denver yesterday—a despatch came saying Cousin Mary's taken worse. And the parsonage is in such a mess still with the painters that I've moved over to the Forest Queen Hotel. But you can come there too—it's kept by an officer's widow, you know, and is most quiet and respectable — and you'll be almost as comfortable waiting there till your transportation comes along as you would be if I could take you home."

Hill said hearing the Forest Queen talked about as quiet and respectable, and Santa Fé's so sort of off-hand making an officer's widow out of old Tenderfoot Sal, set him to shaking at such a rate he had to get to where there was a kag of railroad spikes and set down on it and hold his sides with both hands.

Santa Fé turned to the old gent, Hill said —talking as polite as a Pullman conductor— and told him since he'd been so kind to his unhappy niece he hoped he'd come along with 'em to the hotel too—where he'd be more comfortable, Santa Fé said, getting something to eat and drink than he would be kicking around the deepo waiting till they'd filled in the wash-out and the train could start.

Hill said the Hen give Santa Fé a queer sort of look at that, as much as to ask him if he was dead sure he had the cards for that lead. Santa Fé give her a look back again, as much as to say he knew what was and what wasn't on the table; and then he went on to the old gent, speaking pleasant, telling him likely it might be a little bit noisy over at the hotel—doing her best, he said, Mrs. Major Rogers couldn't help having noise sometimes, things being so rough and tumble out there on the frontier; but he had a private room for his study, where he wrote his sermons, he said, and got into it by a side door—and so he guessed things wouldn't be too bad.

That seemed to make the Hen easy, Hill said; and away the three of 'em went together to the Forest Queen. Hill knowed it

was straight enough about the private room
and the side door—Santa Fé had it to do
business in for himself, on the quiet, when he
didn't have to deal; and Hill 'd known of a
good many folks who'd gone in that private
room by that side door and hadn't come out
again till Santa Fé'd scooped their pile. But
it wasn't no business of his, he said; and he
said he was glad to get shut of 'em so he
might have a chance to let out the laughing
that fairly was hurting his insides.

As they was going away from the deepo,
Hill said, he heard Santa Fé telling the old
gent he was sorry it was getting so dark—as
he'd like to take him round so he could see
the parsonage, and the new church they'd
just finished building and was going to put
an organ in as soon as they'd raised more
funds; but it wasn't worth while going out
of their way, he said, because they wouldn't
show to no sort of advantage with the light
so bad. As the only church in Palomitas was
the Mexican mud one about two hundred
years old, and as the nearest thing to a parsonage was the Padre's house that Denver

The Sage-Brush Hen

Jones had rented and had his faro-bank in, Hill said he guessed Charley acted sensible in not trying to show the old gent around that part of the town.

Hill said after he'd got his supper he thought he'd come down to the deepo and sort of wait around there; on the chance he'd ketch on—when the old gent come over to the train—to what Santa Fé and the Hen 'd been putting up on him. Sure enough, he did.

Along about ten o'clock a starting-order come down—the track-gang by that time having the wash-out so near fixed it would be fit by the time the train got there to go across; and Wood—he was the agent, Wood was—sent word over to the Forest Queen to the old gent, who was the only Pullman passenger, he'd better be coming along.

In five minutes or so he showed up. He wasn't in the best shape, Hill said, and Santa Fé and the Hen each of 'em was giving him an arm; though what he seemed to need more'n arms, Hill said, was legs—

the ones he had, judging from the way he couldn't manage 'em, not being in first-class order and working bad. But he didn't make no exhibition of himself, and talked right enough—only he spoke sort of short and scrappy—and the three of 'em was as friendly together as friendly could be. Hill said he didn't think it was any hurt to listen, things being the way they was, and he edged up close to 'em—while they stood waiting for the porter to light up the Pullman—and though he couldn't quite make sense of all they was saying he did get on to enough of it to size up pretty close how they'd put the old gent through.

"Although it is for my struggling church, a weak blade of grass in the desert," Santa Fé was saying when Hill got the range of 'em, "I cannot but regret having taken from you your splendid contribution to our parish fund in so unusual, I might almost say in so unseemly, a way. That I have returned to you a sufficient sum to enable you to prosecute your journey to its conclusion places you under no obligation to me. Indeed, I

The Sage-Brush Hen

could not have done less—considering the very liberal loan that you have made to my poor niece to enable her to return quickly to her helpless babe. As I hardly need tell you, that loan will be returned promptly—as soon as Mrs. Captain Chiswick gets East and is able to disentangle her affairs."

"Indeed it will," the Hen put in. "My generous benefactor shall be squared with if I have to sell my clothes!"

"Mustn't think of such a thing. Catch cold," the old gent said. "Pleasure's all mine to assist such noble a woman in her unmerited distress. And now I shall have happiness, and same time sorrow, to give her fatherly kiss for farewell."

The Hen edged away a little, Hill said, and Santa Fé shortened his grip a little on the old gent's arm—so his fatherly kissing missed fire. But he didn't seem to notice, and said to Santa Fé: "Never knew a minister know cards like you. Wonderful! And wonderful luck what you held. Played cards a good deal myself. Never could play like you!"

Santa Fé's Partner

Santa Fé steadied the old gent, Hill said, and said to him in a kind of explaining way: "As I told you, my dear sir, in my wild college days—before I got light on my sinful path and headed for the ministry—I was reckoned something out of the common as a card-player; and what the profane call luck used to be with me all the time. Of course, since I humbly—but, I trust, helpfully—took to being a worker in the vineyard, I have not touched those devil's picture-books; nor should I have touched them to-night but for my hope that a little game would help to while away your time of tedious waiting. As for playing for money, that would have been quite impossible had it not been for my niece's suggestion that my winnings—in case such came to me—should be added to our meagre parish fund. I trust that I have not done wrong in yielding to my impulse. At least I have to sustain me the knowledge that if you, my dear sir, are somewhat the worse, my impoverished church is much the better for our friendly game of chance."

Hill said hearing Santa Fé Charley talking

The Sage-Brush Hen

about chance in any game where he had the dealing was so funny it was better'n going to the circus. But the old gent took it right enough — and the Hen added on: "Yes, Uncle Charley can get the organ he's been wanting so badly for his church, now. And I'm sure we'll all think of how we owe its sweet music to you every time we hear it played!"—and she edged up to him again, so he could hold her hand. "It must make you very, very happy, sir," she kept on, speaking kind of low and gentle, but not coming as close as he wanted her, "to go about the world doing such generous-hearted good deeds! I'm sure I'd like to thank you enough—only there aren't any fit words to thank you in—for your noble-hearted generous goodness to me!"

The old gent hauled away on her hand, Hill said, trying to get her closer, and said back to her: "Words quite unnecessary. Old man's heart filled with pleasure obliging such dear child. Never mind about words. Accept old man's fatherly kiss, like daughter, for good-bye."

Santa Fé's Partner

But he missed it that time too, Hill said—
and Hill said, speaking in his careless cuss-
word way, it was pretty damn rough on him
what poor luck in fatherly kisses he seemed
to have—because just then the train conductor swung his lantern and sung out:
"All aboard!"

That ended things. Before the old gent
knowed what had got him, Santa Fé and
the Hen had boosted him up the steps onto
the platform of the Pullman—where the Pullman conductor got a grip on him just in time
to save him from spilling—and then the train
pulled out: with the Pullman conductor keeping him steady, and he throwing back good-
bye kisses to the Hen with both hands.

Hill said the Hen and Santa Fé kept quiet
till the hind-lights showed beyond the end
of the deepo platform: and then the Hen
grabbed Santa Fé round the neck and just
hung onto him—so full of laugh she was limp
—while they both roared. And Hill said he
roared too. It was the most comical bit of
business, he said, he'd tumbled to in all his
born days!

42

The Sage-Brush Hen

It wasn't till the train got clean round the curve above the station, Hill said, that Charley and the Hen could pull 'emselves together so they could talk. Then the Hen let a-go of Santa Fé's neck and said comical— speaking kind of precise and toney, like as if she was an officer's wife sure enough: "You had better return to your study, dear Uncle Charley, and finish writing that sermon you said we'd interrupted you in that was about caring for the sheep as well as the lambs!"

And then they went off together yelling, Hill said, over to the Forest Queen.

III

HART'S NEPHEW'S HOLD-UP

HILL always said he counted on coming into Palomitas some day on one of his mules bareback—leaving the other five dead or stampeded, and the coach stalled somewhere—and bringing his hair only because road-agents hadn't no use for hair and his wasn't easy to get anyhow, he being so bald on top there wasn't nothing to ketch a-hold of if anybody wanted to lift what little there was along the sides. Of course that was just Hill's comical way of putting it; but back of his fool talk there was hard sense—as there was apt to be back of Hill's talk every time. He knew blame well what he was up against, Hill did; and if he hadn't been more'n extra sandy he never could a-held down his job.

Hart's Nephew's Hold-up

Till Hill started his coach up, the only way to get across to Santa Fé from Palomitas was to go a-horseback or walk. Both ways was unhealthy; and the coach, being pretty near as liable to hold-ups, wasn't much healthier. It had to go slow, the coach had —that was a powerful mean road after you left Pojuaque and got in among the sand-hills—and you never was sure when some of them bunches of scrub-cedar wasn't going to wake up and take to pumping lead into you. Only a nervy man, like Hill was, ever could have took the contract; and Hill said he got so rattled sometimes—when it happened he hadn't no passengers and was going it alone in among them sand-hills—he guessed it was only because he had so little hair to turn anything it didn't turn gray.

Hill slept at the Forest Queen, the nights he was in Palomitas — he drove one way one day and the other way the next—and the boys made things cheerfuller for him by all the time rigging him about the poor show he had for sticking long at his job. He'd look well, they said, a-laying out there in the sage-brush plugged full of lead waiting for his friends to call for him; and they asked him how he thought he'd enjoy being a free-lunch counter for coyotes; and they told him he'd better write down on a piece of paper anything he'd like particular to have painted on the board—and they just generally devilled him all round. Hill didn't mind the fool talk they give him—he always was a good-natured fellow, Hill was—and he mostly managed to hit back at 'em, one way or another, so they'd come out about even and end up with drinks for all hands.

The only one who really didn't like that sort of talk, and always kicked when the boys started in on it, was the Sage-Brush Hen. She said it was a mean shame to make a joke about a thing like that, seeing there wasn't a day when it mightn't happen; and it wasn't like an ordinary shooting-match, she said, that come along in the regular way and both of you took your chances; and sometimes she'd get that mad and worried she'd go right smack out of the room.

46

Hart's Nephew's Hold-up

You see, the Hen always thought a heap of Hill—they having got to be such friends together that first day when he brought her over to Palomitas on the coach and helped her put up her rig on the old gent from Washington; and, back of her liking Hill specially, she really was about as good-natured a woman as ever lived. Except Hart's nephew—she did just hate Hart's nephew, who was a chump if ever there was one—she always was as pleasant as pie with everybody; and if any of the boys was hurt—like when Denver Jones got that jag in his shoulder rumpussing with Santa Fé Charley; and she more friends with Charley, of course, than with anybody else—she'd turn right in and help all she knowed how.

But it's a cold fact, for all her being so good-natured and obliging, that wherever that Hen was there was a circus. It was on her account Charley and Denver had their little difficulty; and, one way and another, there was more shooting-scrapes about her than about all the other girls put together in all the dance-halls in town. Why, it got to be so that one corner of the new cemetery out on the mesa was called her private lot. It wasn't her fault, she always said; and, in one way, it wasn't—she always being willing to be sociable and friendly all round. But, all the same, wherever that Sage-Brush Hen was, there was dead sure to be an all-right cyclone.

One night when the boys at the Forest Queen was rigging Hill worse'n usual, and the Hen all the time getting madder and madder, Santa Fé Charley come into the game himself. Knowing how down the Hen was on such doings he usually didn't. I guess he and she'd been having some sort of a ruction that day, and he wanted to get even with her. Anyhow, in he come—and the way he played his hand just got the Hen right up on her ear.

What Charley did was to start a thirty-day pool on Hill as to when it would happen. Chances was a dollar apiece—the dates for thirty days ahead being written on bits of paper, and the bits crumpled up and put

Hart's Nephew's Hold-up

into a hat, and you took one—and the pool
went to whoever got the right date, with
consolation stakes to whoever got the day
before and the day after. Charley made a
comical speech, after the drawing, telling
the boys it was what you might call a quick
return investment, and he guessed all of
'em had got left who'd drawed dates more'n
a week away. Hill took it all right, same
as usual; and just to show 'em he didn't
bear no malice he bought a chance himself. He was one of the best-natured fellows ever got born, Hill was. There wasn't
no Apache in him nowhere. He was white
all the way through. So he bought his
chance, that way, and then he give it to
the Hen — telling her if he pulled the pot
himself it wouldn't be much good to him,
and saying he hoped she'd get it if anybody did, and asking her — if she did get
it—to have some extry nice touches put on
the board.

Well, will you believe it? When Hill give
that Hen his chance she begun to cry over
it! She knew it wouldn't do to cry hard—

seeing what a mess it would make with her color when the tears got running—and so she pulled herself up quick and mopped her eyes dry with her pocket-handkerchief. And then she let out with all four legs at once, like a Colorado mule, and everlastingly gave it to all hands! It was just like the Hen, being so good-hearted, and thinking so much of Hill, to fire up like that about Santa Fé's pool on when he'd get his medicine; and all the boys knowed that beside the address she was making to the whole congregation Santa Fé was going to get another, and a worse one, when she had him off where she could play out to him a lone hand. But the boys didn't mind the jawing she give 'em—except they was a little ashamed, knowing putting such a rig on Hill was a mean thing to do— and I guess the whole business would have ended right there (only for the dressing-down Santa Fé was to get later) if Hart's nephew hadn't taken it into his head to chip in—being drunker'n usual, and a fool anyway—and so started what turned out to be a fresh game.

I do suppose Hart's nephew was about

Hart's Nephew's Hold-up

the meanest ever got born. Bill Hart was
a good enough fellow himself, and how he
ever come to have such a God-forsaken
chump for a nephew was more'n anybody
could tell. Things must have been powerful bad, I reckon, on his mother's side. He
was one of the blowing kind, with nothing
behind his blow; and his feet was that tender
they wasn't fit to walk on anything harder'n
fresh mush. The boys all the time was putting up rigs on him; and he'd go around
talking so big about what he meant to do to
get even with 'em you'd think he was going
to clean out the whole town. But he took
mighty good care to do his tall talking pro-
miscuous: after making the mistake of trying it once on a little man he thought he
could manage—a real peaceable little feller
that looked like he wouldn't stand up to a
kitten—and getting his nose and his mouth
and his eyes all mashed into one. The little
man apologized to the rest for doing it that
way, saying he'd a-been ashamed of himself
all the rest of his life if he'd gone for a thing
like that with his gun.

Santa Fé's Partner

Well, it was this Hart's nephew — like enough he had some sort of a name that belonged to him, but he wasn't worth the trouble of finding out what it was — who chipped in when the Hen took to her tirading, and so give things a new turn. Standing up staggery, and talking in his drunk fool way, he told her the road across to Santa Fé was as safe as a Sunday-school; and he said he'd be glad to be in Hill's boots and drive that coach himself, seeing what an interest she took in stage-drivers; and he asked her, sort of nasty, how she managed to get along for company when Hill was at the other end of his run. Hart's nephew was drunker'n usual that night, same as I've said, or even he'd a-knowed he'd likely get into trouble talking that way to the Hen.

For about a minute things looked real serious. The Hen straightened right up, and on the back of her neck — where it showed, she not being fixed red there to start with—she got as red as canned tomatoes; and some of the boys moved a little, sort of uneasy; and Santa Fé reached out

Hart's Nephew's Hold-up

over the piles of chips for his gun. He didn't
get it, because the Hen saw what he was
doing and stopped him by looking at him
quick—and knowing what Charley was when
it come to shooting, you'll know the Hen
sent that look at him about as fast as looks
can go! The game had stopped right there;
and it was so quiet in the room you'd a-
thought the snoring of the two drunks asleep
on benches in one corner was a thunder-storm
coming down the cañon!

Of course what we all expected the Hen
to do was to wipe up the floor with Hart's
nephew by giving him such a talking to—she
could use language, the Hen could, when she
started in at it—as would make him sorrier'n
usual he'd ever been born; and I guess, from
the looks of her, that was what at the first
jump she meant to do. But she was a quick-
thinking one, the Hen was, and she had a
way of getting more funny notions into that
good-looking head of hers than any other
woman that ever walked around on this earth
alive—and so she give us all a real jolt by
playing out cards we wasn't expecting at all.

53

Santa Fé's Partner

Just as sudden as a wink, she sort of twitched and twinkled—same as she always did when she was up to some new bit of deviltry—and when she set her stamps to going she talked like as if she was real pleased. She didn't look, though, as good-natured as she talked —keeping on being straightened up, and having a kind of setness in her jaws and a snappiness in them big black eyes of hers that made everybody but Hart's nephew, who was too drunk to know anything, dead sure she still was mad all the way through.

"If he'll lend 'em to you, and I guess he will, why don't you get into Mr. Hill's boots?" she said to Hart's nephew. And then she fetched up a nice sort of smile, and said to him real friendly-sounding: "I do like stage-drivers, and that's a fact — and there's no telling how pleasant I'll make things for you if you'll take the coach across to Santa Fé to-morrow over that Sunday-school road! Will you do it?" And then the Hen give him one of them fetching looks of hers, and asked him over: "Will you do it—to oblige *me ?*"

Hart's Nephew's Hold-up

Now that was more words at one time than the Hen had dropped on Hart's nephew since he struck the camp; and as the few he'd ever got from her mostly hadn't been nice ones, and these sounding to him—he being drunk —like as if they was real good-natured, he was that pleased he didn't know what to do. Of course he was dead set on the Hen, same as everybody else was — she truly was a powerful fine woman—and it just was funny to see how he tried to steady himself on his legs gentlemanly, and was all over fool smiles.

So he said back to the Hen—speaking slow, to keep his words from tumbling all over each other—he'd just drive that coach across to Santa Fé a-hooping if Hill'd lend it to him; and then he asked Hill if he might have it— and told him he could trust him to handle it in good shape, because everybody knowed he was a real daisy at driving mules.

For a fact, Hart's nephew did manage well at mule-driving. It was one of the blame few things that fool knowed how to do. Denver Jones allowed it was because he was related to 'em—on the father's side.

55

Santa Fé's Partner

"Just for this once, Mr. Hill," said the Hen, speaking coaxy. And she got her head round a little—so Hart's nephew couldn't see what she was doing—and give Hill a wink to come into the game.

Hill didn't know what in the world the Hen was up to—nobody ever did know what that Hen was up to when once she got started —but he reckoned he could take it back in the morning if he didn't think what she wanted would answer, so in he come: telling Hart's nephew he might have the coach to do anything (Hill was a kind of a careless talker) he damn pleased with; and saying he'd have it hitched up and ready down at the deepo next morning, same as usual, so he could start right off when the Denver train come in.

When things was settled, all quick that way, Hart's nephew took to squirming—he seeing, drunk as he was, he'd bit off a blame sight more'n he cared to chew. But with the Hen right after him—and Hill and all the rest of the boys backing her, they being sure she'd dandy cards up her sleeve for the queer

56

Hart's Nephew's Hold-up

game she was playing — he couldn't make
nothing by all his squirms. The boys got at
him and told him anybody could see he was
afraid; and the Hen got at him and told him
anybody could see he wasn't, and she said
she knew he was about the bravest man
alive; and Hill got at him and told him the
road had improved so, lately, the nearest to
road-agents you ever seen on it was burros
and cotton-tail rabbits; and all of 'em together kept getting more drinks in him right
along. So the upshot of it was: first Hart's
nephew stopped his squirming; and then he
took to telling what a holy wonder he was at
mule-driving; and then he went to blowing
the biggest kind—till he got so he couldn't
talk no longer—about what he'd do in the
shooting line if any road-agents come around
trying their monkey-shine hold-ups on *him!*
So it ended, good enough, by their getting
him fixed tight in his hole.

ᵥ The boys kept things going with him pretty
late that night, and when he showed up in
the morning at the deepo—a delegation seeing to it he got there, and Hill having the

57

coach all ready for him—he still had on him a fairly sizable jag. But he'd sobered up enough — having slept quite a little, and soaked his head at the railroad tank — to want to try all he knew how to spill himself out of his job. It took all the Hen could do —the Hen had got up early and come down to the deepo a-purpose to attend to him— and all the boys could do helping her, to get him up on that coach-box and boosted off out of town.

He was that nervous he was shaking all over; and what made him nervouser was having no passengers—nobody for Santa Fé having come in on the Denver train. It was just a caution to see his shooting outfit! The box of the coach looked like it was a gun-shop—being piled up with two Winchesters and a double-barrelled shot-gun (the shot-gun, he said, was to cripple anybody he didn't think it was needful to kill); and beside that he had a machete some Mexican lent him hooked on to his belt, and along with it a brace of derringers and two forty-fives. Hill was the only one who didn't

Hart's Nephew's Hold-up

laugh fit to kill himself over that lay-out. Hill said Hart's nephew done just right to take along all the guns he could get a-hold of; and Hill said he'd attended to the proper loading of every one of them weepons himself.

At last—with all the boys laughing away and firing fool talk at him, and the Hen keeping him up to the collar by going on about how brave he was—he did manage to whip up his mules and start off. Sick was no name for him—and he was so scared stiff he looked like he was about ready to cry. After he'd got down the slope, and across the bridge over the Rio Grande, and was walking his mules on that first little stretch of sandy road on the way to La Cañada, we could see him reaching down and fussing over his lay-out of guns.

For a cold fact, there was a right smart chance that Hart's nephew—and 'specially because his fool luck made most things come to him contrairy—really might run himself into a hold-up; and, if he did, it was like as not his chips might get called in. For all

Santa Fé's Partner

Hill's funny talk about meeting nothing worse'n burros and cotton-tail rabbits, that road was a bad road—and things was liable to occur. Hill himself was taking his chances, and he blame well knowed it, every day. But it was the sense of the meeting that if a hold-up of that coach attended by fatalities was coming, it couldn't come at a better time than when Hart's nephew was on the box—the feeling being general that Hart's nephew was one that could be spared. I guess Bill Hart felt just the same about it as the rest of us — leastways, he didn't strain himself any trying to keep his nephew home.

Things went kind of nervous that day at Palomitas. All the boys seemed to have a feeling, somehow, there was going to be happenings; and we all just sort of idled round waiting for 'em—taking more drinks 'n usual, and in spite of the drinks getting every minute lower and lower in our minds. Except the day Hart's aunt spent with him, and Santa Fé Charley run the kindergarten, I reckon it was the quietest day we ever went through—at least till we got along to the clean-up that turned Palomitas into what some of us felt was a blame sight too much of a Sunday-school town.

One reason why we all was so serious was because the Sage-Brush Hen—who started most of what happened—didn't show up as usual; and all hands got a real jolt when some of the boys went off to the Forest Queen to ask about her, and old Tenderfoot Sal told 'em she was laying down in her room and wasn't feeling well. The Hen being always an out-and-out hustler, and hard as an Indian pony, her not being well shook us up bad. Everybody was friends with her, same as she was friends with everybody—even when she got into one of her tantrums, and took to jawing you, you couldn't help liking her—and knowing she wasn't feeling like she ought to feel put a big lot more of a damper on all hands. So we just kept on taking drinks and getting miserabler with 'em—and feeling all the time surer something was coming bouncing out at us from round the corner, and wondering what kind of a stir-up we was likely to have.

Santa Fé's Partner

It was along about four o'clock in the afternoon the cyclone struck us; and it was such a small-sized one, when we did get it, we didn't know whether to laugh or swear. But the cyclone himself didn't think there was anything small about him: being Hart's nephew—so scared to death all the few wits he ever had was knocked clean out of him—who come into Palomitas, white as white-wash, riding bareback one of the coach mules.

He just sort of rolled off the mule, in front of the Forest Queen, and went in to the bar and got four drinks in him before he could speak a word—and then he said he'd been held up at the Barranca Grande by about two hundred road-agents who'd opened up on him and killed all the mules except the one he'd got away on; and his getting away at all, he said, was only because he'd put up such a fight he'd scared 'em—and after that because they couldn't hit him when once he was off, and had the mule going on a dead run. Then he took two more drinks, and told his story all over again; and as it was

Hart's Nephew's Hold-up

about the same story both times—and he so
scared, and by the time he told it over again
so set up with his drinks, it didn't seem
likely he'd sense enough left to be lying—
the boys allowed like enough it was true.

What he had to tell—except he piled on
more road-agents than was needed—was
about reasonable. He said he'd done well
enough as far as Pojuaque—where he'd had
his dinner and changed mules, same as usual,
at old man Bouquet's. And after he'd left
Pojuaque he'd got along all right, he said,
except he had to go slow through the sand-
hills, till he come to the Barranca Grande.

It's a bad place, that barranca is. The
road goes sharp down into it, and then sharp
up out of it—and both banks so steep you
want all the brakes you've got to get to the
bottom of it, and more mules than you're
likely to have to get to the top on the other
side.

Well, Hart's nephew said he'd just got the
coach down to the bottom of the barranca—
he'd took the last of the slope at a run, he
said, and was licking away at his mules for

all he was worth to start 'em up the far side—
when the road-agents opened on him, being
hid in among the cedar-bushes, from the
top of the bank and from both sides of the
trail. You never seen such a blaze of shooting in all your life, Hart's nephew said; and
he said before he'd a chance to get a gun up
all his mules was hit but one. He said he
jumped quick from the box, taking both
Winchesters and the shot-gun with him,
and having his guns and the derringers in his
belt beside, and got behind the one mule that
hadn't been downed and opened up on the
bushes where the smoke was and let go as
hard as he knowed how. He said he must
a-killed more'n twenty of 'em, he guessed,
judging by the yelling and groaning, and by
the way they slacked up on their fire. Their
slacking that way give him a chance, he said,
and he took it—cutting the mule loose from
the harness with one hand, while he kept on
blazing away over her back with the other;
then letting 'em have it from both hands for
a minute, from what guns he had left that
wasn't empty, to sort of paralyze 'em; and

64

then getting quick on the mule's back and starting her down the barranca on a dead run.

He had balls buzzing all about him, he said, till he got out of sight around a turn in the barranca; and he said before he made that turn he looked back once and saw a big feller up on top of the bank letting off at him as hard as he could go. Just to show he still had fight in him, he said, he let off back at him with his two derringers—which was all he had left to shoot with—and he was pretty sure, though of course it was only luck did it with the mule bouncing him so, the big feller went down. He was a tremendous tall man, he said; and he guessed he was a Greaser, seeing he had a big black beard and was dressed in Greaser clothes.

He said he didn't mind owning up he was scared bad while he was in it; but he said he guessed anybody would a-been scared with all them fellers shooting away at him—and, as he'd made as good a fight of it as he knowed how, he didn't think he was to be blamed for ending by running from such a crowd. He kept on down the barranca for about two miles, he said, till he struck the cross-trail to Tesuque; and he headed north on that till he got to Pojuaque—where he give the mule a rest, she was blowed all to bits, the mule was, he said; and he got some of old man Bouquet's wine in him, feeling pretty well blowed to bits himself; and then he come along home.

Well, that seemed a straight enough story. The only thing in it you really could pick on—except the number of road-agents, he only having seen one, and the rest being his scared guesswork—was the mule not being hit while he was doing all that firing over the back of her. But all fights has their queer chances in 'em; and that was a chance that might a-happened, same as others. Of course, the one big general thing that didn't seem likely was that such a runt as Hart's nephew should have stood up the way he said he did to as much as one road-agent—let alone to the half-dozen or so that like enough had got at him. But even a thing like Hart's nephew sometimes will put up a fight when it's scared so bad it really don't more'n half know what it's doing—and the boys allowed he might have done his fighting that way.

That the size of his scare had been big enough to make him do a'most anything showed up from the way he kept on being scared after it was all over—he coming into Palomitas looking like a wet white rag when, by his own showing, he'd been out of reach of anybody's hurting him for four or five hours anyway, and had had a chance to cool off at Pojuaque while he was loading in old man Bouquet's wine. And so, taking the story by and large, the boys allowed that likely most of it was true; and some of 'em even went so far as to say maybe Hart's nephew wasn't more'n half rotten, after all.

It was a good story to hear, anyway; and everybody was sorry the Hen wasn't around to hear it. But when some of the boys tried to rout her out, Tenderfoot Sal stood 'em off savage—telling 'em to go about their business, and the Hen's head was aching bad. So the boys had to take it out in

making Hart's nephew keep on telling all
he had to tell over and over; and he was glad
of the chance to, and did—till he got so
many drinks in him he couldn't tell anything;
and then his uncle, with Shorty Smith helping, took him off home.

Next morning, having pretty much slept
himself sober, Hart's nephew went cavorting
around Palomitas—that little runt did—like
he was about ten foot tall! He had the whole
thing over, in the course of the day, a dozen
times or more; and as he kept on telling
it—now he was sober enough to add things
on — it got to be about the biggest fight
with road-agents that ever was. The thing
that was biggest was the one man he allowed
he'd really seen. Why, Goliath of Gath
wasn't in it with that fellow, according to
Hart's nephew! And he was that desperate
and dangerous to look at, he said, not many
men would a-had the nerve to try at him
with only a derringer—and, what was more,
to bring him down. It was well along in the
afternoon before we got it for a fact that

Hart's Nephew's Hold-up

Hart's nephew really had killed the Greaser. The thing growed that way—from his first telling how he thought he'd hit him—until it ended with the Greaser giving a yell like a stuck pig; and then staggering and throwing his arms up; and then rolling over and over down the side of the barranca to the bottom of it—with his goose cooked all the way through!

We was all down at the deepo waiting for the Denver train to pull out, same as usual, while Hart's nephew was doing his tallest talking—and while he was hard at it somebody jumped up and sung out the Santa Fé coach was coming along on the other side of the river from Santa Cruz. Well, that was about the last thing anybody was expecting—and everybody hustled up off the barrels and boxes where they was a-setting and looked with all their eyes.

Sure enough, there the old coach was—just as it always was, about that time of day—coming along as natural as you please. After a while, it keeping on getting nearer, we could see it was old Hill himself up on the

69

box driving his mules in good shape; and
when he got along near the bridge we could
hear him swearing at 'em — Hill did use
terrible bad language to them mules — in
just his ordinary way. Then he rattled the
mules over the bridge and brought 'em a-
clipping up the slope this side of it; and then
in another minute he pulled right up at the
deepo platform where we all was. Hill was
laughing all over as he come up to us, and so
was a Mexican who was setting on the box
with him—a nice tidy little chap, with a
powerful big black beard on him—and Hill
sung out: "Have you boys heard about the
hold-up?" And then he and the little
Mexican got to laughing so it was a wonder
they didn't fall off.

Nobody was thinking nothing about Hart's
nephew—till he let off a yell and sung out:
"That's the man held the coach up! Get a
bead on him with your guns!" And he got
his own gun out—and like enough would
a-done some fool thing with it if Santa Fé
Charley, who was right by him, hadn't
smacked him and jerked it out of his hand.

Hart's Nephew's Hold-up

Santa Fé smacked so's to hurt him; and he put his hand up to his face and said, kind of whimpery: "What are you hitting me like that for, Charley? I ain't done nothing. I tell you that man on the box with Hill is the one I was held up by yesterday. He's dangerous. If we don't get a-hold of him quick he'll be doing something to us with his gun!" And Hart's nephew a'most broke out crying—being all worked up, and Santa Fé having smacked him blame hard.

At that, Denver Jones cut in with: "I thought you said the one you was held up by was more'n fourteen foot high, and you killed him? This man ain't big enough to hold up a baby-carriage with you in it— and he's sure enough alive. What are you giving us—you blame fool?"

There's no telling what kind of an answer Denver would a-got from Hart's nephew— for he hadn't a chance to give him no answer at all. Just then Hill did the talking, and what Hill said was: "Boys, he's dead right about it. This here's the bad man that held the coach up—and as I was there, and seen it done, and drove the coach on with five mules to Santa Fé afterwards, I guess I know!" And Hill, and the little Mexican with him, just roared.

When Hill could talk for laughing, he went on: "I'll own up right now, boys, I was extry over-precautious when I fixed up with empty shells that gun-shop Hart's nephew took along on the coach when he started out with it. For all the harm he done with them guns, I might just as well a-left 'em loaded the usual way. He was that scared when this here gigantic ruffian stopped him—I just happened to be a-setting in among the cedar-bushes at the time, smoking a seegar and looking on sort of casual—he couldn't do nothing more'n yell out he wasn't going to shoot, and not to murder him; and then down he jumped from the box—me a-smoking away looking at him, and this here ruffian a-shooting his Winchester across the top of the coach to where he said he thought he seen a jack-rabbit—and cut out the near wheeler; and then he scrambled up anyhow on that mule's back, and away he went down

Hart's Nephew's Hold-up

the barranca as hard as hell!" (Hill oughtn't
to have said that word. But he was careless
in his talk, Hill was, and he did).

"But Hart's nephew being scared that
way," Hill went on, a'most choking, "don't
count one way or the other when you get
down to the facts. It was this here dangerous
devil that done that wicked deed, and he done
it all alone by his dangerous self. At the
risk of my life, gentlemen, I've got a-hold of
him to bring him to justice, and here he is.
And I guess the sooner we yank him up to
the usual telegraph-pole, and so get shut of
him, the sooner it 'll be safe for folks to trav-
el these roads. He's the most dangerous I
ever see," said Hill, and by that time Hill
was so near busted with his laughing he was
purple; "and what makes him such a particular holy terror is he goes disguised!"
And then—choking so he could hardly speak
plain—Hill whipped round to the little Mexican and says to him: "Get your disguise
off of you, you murdersome critter! Get it
off, I say, and give these gentlemen a look
at the terrible wicked face of you—before

73

you and that telegraph-pole gets to being friends!"

And then the little Mexican switched his big black beard off—and right smack there before us was the Sage - Brush Hen! You never heard such a yell as the boys give in all your born days!

And you never in all your born days saw such goings on as there was that night at the Forest Queen! Everybody in Palomitas was right there. The other banks and bars hadn't a soul left in 'em but the dealers and the drink - slingers — and they, not having nothing to do at home, just shut up shop and come along too. All the girls from all the dance-halls showed up, the Hen being real down popular with 'em—which told well for her—and they wanting to see the fun. Cherry happened to be down from his ranch that night; and Becker got wind of what was up and footed it across from Santa Cruz de la Cañada; and word was sent to the Elbogen brothers—they was real clever young fellows, them two Germans—and over they come

Hart's Nephew's Hold-up

a-kiting on their buck-board from San Juan.
I guess it was about the biggest jam the Forest
Queen ever had.

Hart's nephew was the only one around
the place who hung back a little, but he got
there all right—being fished out of an empty
flour-barrel, where he'd hid under the counter
in his uncle's store, and brought along by the
invitation committee sent to look for him all
dabbed over with flour.

Some thought the way they used Hart's
nephew that night was just a little mite too
hard lines—he not being let to have as much
as a single drink in him, and so kept plumb
sober while the Hen give him his medicine;
but all hands allowed—after his sassy talk to
her—he didn't get no more'n she'd a right to
give. She just went at him like a blister, the
Hen did; and she blistered him worse because
she did it in her own funny way—telling him
she did just dote on stage-drivers, and if he
really wanted to please her he'd take Hill's
job regular; and leading the boys up to him
and introducing him, lady-like, as "the hold-
up hero"; and asking him to please to tell her

all about that fourteen-foot road-agent he'd killed; and just rubbing the whole thing in on him every way she knowed how. Before the Hen got done with him he was about the sickest man, Hart's nephew was, you ever seen! But I guess it learned him quite a little about how when he talked to ladies he'd better be polite.

Fun wasn't no name that night for that Hen! She kept on wearing her Mexican clothes, and she did look real down cute in 'em; and she'd got a God-forsaken old rusty pepper-box six-shooter from somewheres, and went flourishing it about saying it was what she'd held up the coach with; and in between times, when she wasn't deviling Hart's nephew, she'd go round the room drawing beads on the boys with her pepper-box, and making out she was dangerous by putting her big black beard on, and standing up in attitudes so the boys might see, she said, how road-agency she looked and bad and bold! Why, the Hen did act so comical that night all hands pretty near died with their laugh!

IV

W HEN Bill Hart, who was a good fellow and kept the principal store in Palomitas, got word his aunt in Vermont was coming out to pay him a visit —it being too late to stop her, and he knowing he'd have to worry the thing through somehow till he could start her back East again—he was the worst broke-up man you ever seen.

"Great Scott! Joe," Hart said, when he was telling Cherry about it, "Palomitas ain't no sort of a town to bring aunts to—and it's about the last town I know of where Aunt Maria 'll fit in! She's the old-fashioned kind, right up to the limit, Aunt Maria is. Sewing-societies and Sunday-schools is the hands she

77

holds flushes in; and she has the preacher
once a week to supper; and when it comes
to kindergartens—Hart was so worked up
he talked careless—she's simply hell! What's
a woman like that going to do, I want to
know, in a place like this — that's mainly
made up of saloons and dance-halls and faro-
banks, and everybody mostly drunk, and
shooting-scrapes going on all the time? It
just makes me sick to think about it." And
Hart groaned.

Cherry swore for a while, sort of friendly
and sociable—he was a sympathetic man,
Cherry was, and always did what he could
to help—and as Hart was too far gone to
swear for himself, in a way that amounted
to anything, hearing what Cherry had to
say seemed to do him good.

"I'd stop her, if there was any stop to
her," he went on, in a minute or two, speaking hopeless and miserable; "but there ain't.
She says she's starting the day after she
writes—having a chance to come sudden with
friends—and that means she's most here
now. And there's no heading her off—be-

Santa Fé Charley's Kindergarten

cause she says the friends she's hooked fast to may be coming to Pueblo and may be coming to Santa Fé. But it don't make any difference, she says, as she's told she can get down easy by the railroad from Pueblo, or she can slide across to Palomitas by 'a short and pleasant coach-ride'—that's what she calls it—from Santa Fé.

"That's all she tells about her coming. The rest of what's in her letter is about how glad she'll be to see me, and about how glad she knows I'll be to see her—being lonely so far from my folks, and likely needing my clothes mended, and pleased to be eating some of her home-made pies. It's just like Aunt Maria to put in things like that. You see, she brought me up—and she's never got out of her head I'm more'n about nine years old. What I feel like doing is going out in the sage-brush and blowing the top of my fool head off, and letting the coyotes eat what's left of me and get me out of the way!"

Hart really did look as if he meant it, Cherry said afterwards. He was the miserablest looking man, he said, he'd ever seen alive.

Cherry said he begun to have a notion, though, while Hart was talking, how the thing might be worked so there wouldn't be no real trouble if it could be fixed so Hart's aunt wouldn't stay in Palomitas more'n about a day; and he come right on down to the Forest Queen to see if he could get the boys to help him put it through. He left Hart clearing out the room he kept flour and meal in—being the cleanest—trying to rig up for his aunt some sort of a bunking-place. He was going to give her his own cot and mattress, he said; and he could fit her out with a looking-glass and a basin and pitcher all right because he kept them sort of things to sell; and he said he'd make the place extra tidy by putting a new horse-blanket on the floor. Seeing his way to getting a grip on that much of the contract, Cherry said, seemed to make him feel a little less bad.

Cherry waited till the deal was over, when he got to the Forest Queen; and then he asked Santa Fé Charley if he'd let him speak

Santa Fé Charley's Kindergarten

to the boys for a minute before the game
went on. He was always polite and obliging,
Santa Fé was, and he said of course he might;
and he rapped on the table with his derringer for order, and said Mr. Cherry had the
floor. Charley was old-fashioned in his ways
of fighting. He always had a six-shooter in
his belt, same as other folks; but he said he
kept it mainly for show. Derringers, he said,
was better and surer — because you could
work 'em around in your pocket while the
other fellow was getting his gun out, and
before he was ready for business you could
shoot him right through your pants. Later
on, it was that very way Santa Fé shot Hart.
But he always was friendly with Hart till
he did shoot him; and it was more his backing than anything else—'specially when it
come to the kindergarten—that made Cherry's plan for helping Hart out go through.

When the game was stopped, and the boys
was all listening, Cherry told about the hole
Hart was in and allowed it was a deep one;
and he said it was only fair—Hart having
done good turns for most everybody, one

time and another — his friends should be
willing to take some trouble to get him out
of it. Hart's aunt, he said, come from a
quiet part of Vermont, and likely would be
jolted bad when she struck Palomitas if
things was going the ordinary way—she being elderly, and like enough a little set in her
ways, and not used much to crazy drunks,
and shooting-matches, and such kinds of
lively carryings-on. But she'd only stay one
day, or at most a day and a half—Hart having agreed to take her right back East himself, if she couldn't be got rid of no other
way—and that gave 'em a chance to fix
things so her feelings wouldn't be hurt,
though doing it was going to be hard on all
hands. And then, having got the boys
worked up wondering what he was driving
at, Cherry went ahead and said he wanted
'em to agree—just for the little while Hart's
aunt was going to stay there—to run Palomitas like it was a regular back-East Sunday-
school town. He knew he was asking a good
deal, he said, but he did ask it—and he ap-
pealed to the better feelings of the gentlemen

Santa Fé Charley's Kindergarten

assembled around that faro-table to do that
much to get Bill Hart out of his hole.   Then
Cherry said he wasn't nobody's orator, but
he guessed he'd made clear what he wanted
to lay before the meeting; and he said he was
much obliged, and had pleasure in setting up
drinks for the crowd.

As was to be expected of 'em, all the boys
—knowing Hart for a square-acting man,
and liking him—tumbled right off to Cherry's
plan.   Santa Fé said—this was after they'd
had their drinks—he s'posed he was chairman of the meeting, and he guessed he spoke
the sense of the meeting when he allowed
Mr. Cherry's scheme was about the only way
out for their esteemed fellow-citizen, Mr.
Hart, and it ought to go through.   But as
it was a matter that seriously affected the
comfort and convenience of everybody in
Palomitas, he said, it was only square to
take a vote on it—and so he'd ask all in
favor of Mr. Cherry's motion to say "Ay."
And everybody in the room—except the few
that was asleep, or too drunk to say anything
—said "Ay" as loud as they knowed how.

. 83

Santa Fé's Partner

"Mr. Cherry's motion is carried, gentle-men," Santa Fé said; "and I will now ap-point a committee to draught a notice to be posted at the deepo, and to call around at the other banks and saloons in the town and notify verbally our fellow-citizens of the action we have taken—and I will ask the Hen here kindly to inform the other ladies of Palomitas of our intentions, and to request their assistance in realizing them. She had better tell them, I reckon, that the way they can come to the front most effectively in this crisis is by keeping entirely out of sight in the rear."

The Sage-Brush Hen, along with some of the other girls, had come in from the back room—where the dancing was—to find out what the circus was about; and when they caught on to what Palomitas was going to be like when Hart's aunt struck it they all just yelled.

"You've come out well once as the Baptist minister, Charley," the Hen said, shaking all over; "and I reckon you can do it again—only it won't be so easy showing off the new

"WROTE OUT A NOTICE THAT WAS TACKED UP ON THE DEEPO
DOOR"

Santa Fé Charley's Kindergarten

church and the parsonage by daylight as it
was in the dark. About us girls laying low,
maybe you're right and maybe you're not
right. Anyway, don't you worry about us.
All I'll say is, it won't be the ladies in this
combine that 'll give anything away!" And
she and the other girls got so to laughing over
it they all of 'em had to set down.

Cherry was more pleased than a little the
way things had gone—and he said so to the
boys, and set up drinks all round again.
Then he and Abe Simons—they was the committee to do it—wrote out a notice that was
tacked up on the deepo door and read this
way:

TO THE CITIZENS OF PALOMITAS

Mr. William Hart's aunt is coming to
pay him a visit, and will strike this town
either by the Denver train to-morrow
morning or the Santa Fé coach to-morrow
afternoon.

She is a perfect lady, and it is ordered
that during her stay in Palomitas this
town has got to behave itself so her feelings won't be hurt. She is to be took
care of and given a pleasant impression.
All fights and drunks must be put off till

she's gone. Persons neglecting to do so
will be taken out into the sage-brush by
members of the committee, and are likely
to get hurt.

Mr. Hart regrets this occurrence as
much as anybody, and agrees his aunt's
visit sha'n't last beyond a day and a half
if she comes down from Denver, and only
one day if she comes in from Santa Fé.

(*Signed*) THE COMMITTEE.

When Cherry got a-hold of Hart and told
him what the town had agreed to do for him
he was that grateful—being all worked up,
anyway—he pretty near cried.

As it turned out, Hart's aunt come in on
Hill's coach from Santa Fé—her friends having gone down that way by the Atchison—
and as Hill had been at the meeting at the
Forest Queen he was able to give things a
good start. Hill always was a friendly sort
of a fellow, and—except he used terrible bad
language, which he said come of his having
to drive mules—he was a real first-class
ladies' man.

Hill said he spotted Hart's aunt the minute

Santa Fé Charley's Kindergarten

he set his eyes on her waiting for the coach at the Fonda, there not being likely to be more'n one in the Territory of that kind. She was a trig little old lady, dressed up in black clothes as neat as wax, he said, with a little black bonnet setting close to her head; and she wore gold specs and had a longish nose. But she'd a real friendly look about her, he said; and while she spoke a little precise and particular she wasn't a bit stuck-up, and seemed to be taking things about as they happened to come along. When he asked her if she wouldn't set up on the box with him, so she could see the country, she said that was just what would suit her; and up she come, he said, as spry as a queer little bird. Then he whipped up his mules—being careful not to use any language—and got the coach started, and begun right off to be agreeable by telling her he guessed he had the pleasure of knowing her nephew, and asking her if she wasn't the aunt of Mr. William Hart.

Well, of course that set things to going pleasant between 'em; and when she'd

allowed she was Hart's aunt, and said she
was glad to meet a friend of his, she started
in asking all the questions about Bill and
about Palomitas she knowed how to ask.

Hill said he guessed that day they had to
lay off the regular recording angel and put
a hired first-class stenographer on his job—
seeing how no plain angel, not writing short-
hand, could a-kept up with all the lies he
felt it his duty to tell if he was going to
bring Bill through in good shape and keep
up the reputation of the town. It wasn't
square to charge them lies up to him, anyway, Hill said, seeing he only was playing
Cherry's hand for him; and he said he hoped
they was put in Cherry's bill. By the time
he'd got through with his fairy tales, he said,
he'd give Hart such a character he didn't
know him himself; and he'd touched up
Palomitas till he'd got it so it might a-been
a town just outside Boston—only he allowed
they was sometimes troubled with hard cases
passing through; and he told her of course
she'd find things kind of half-baked and noisy
out there on the frontier. And she must re-

Santa Fé Charley's Kindergarten

member, he told her, that all the folks in the
town was young—young men who'd brought
their young wives with 'em, come to hustle
in a new country—and she mustn't mind if
things went livelier 'n the way she was used
to back East.

Hill said she said she wasn't expecting to
find things like they was at home, and she
guessed she'd manage all right—seeing she
always got on well with young people, and
wasn't a bit set in her own ways.   And she
said she was as pleased as she was surprised
to find out the kind of a town Palomitas was
—because her nephew William's letters had
led her to think it had a good many bad
characters in it;   and he'd not mentioned
any church but the Catholic one where the
natives went; and as to the Bible Class and the
Friendly Aid Society, he'd never said a word
about 'em at all.   She went on talking so
cheerful and pleasant, Hill said, it give him
creeps in his back; and he got so rattled the
last half of the run—coming on from Pojuaque, where they'd had dinner at old man
Bouquet's—he hardly knowed what he'd told

and what he hadn't, and whether he was standing on his head or his heels.

Being that way, he made the only break that gave trouble afterwards. She asked him if there was a school in Palomitas, and he told her there wasn't, because all the folks in town was so young—except the natives, who hadn't no use for schools—they hadn't any children big enough to go to one. And then she said sudden, and as it seemed to him changing the subject: "Isn't there a kindergarten?" Hill said he'd never heard tell of such a concern; but he sized it up to be some sort of a fancy German garden—like the one Becker'd fixed up for himself over to Santa Cruz—and he said he allowed, from the way she asked about it, it was what Palomitas ought to have. So he told her there was, and it was the best one in the Territory—and let it go at that. He said she said she was glad to hear it, as she took a special interest in kindergartens, and she'd go and see it the first thing.

Hill said he knowed he'd put his foot in it somehow; but as he didn't know how he'd put his foot in it, he just switched her off by telling her about the Dorcas Society. He had the cards for that, he said, because his mother'd helped run a Dorcas Society back East and he knowed what he was talking about. The Palomitas one met Thursdays, he told her, at the Forest Queen. That was the principal hotel, he told her, and was kept by Mrs. Major Rogers, who was an officer's widow and had started the society to make clothes for some of the Mexican poor folks— and he said it was a first-rate charity and worked well. It tickled him so, he said, thinking of any such doings at the Forest Queen—with old Tenderfoot Sal, of all people, bossing the job!—he had to work off the laugh he had inside of him by taking to licking his mules.

But it went all right with the little old lady; and she was that interested he had to strain himself, he said, making up more stories about it—till by good luck she took to telling him about the Dorcas Society she belonged to herself, back home in Vermont; and was so full of it she kept things going easy for him till they'd crossed the bridge over the Rio Grande and was coming up the slope into the town at a walk.

Up at the top of the slope Santa Fé Charley stood a-waiting for 'em—looking, of course, in them black clothes and a white tie on, like he was a sure-enough preacher—and as the coach come along he sung out, pleasant and friendly: "Good-afternoon, Brother Hill. I missed you at the Bible Class last evening. No doubt you were detained unavoidably, and it's all right. But be sure to come next Friday. We don't get along well without you, Brother Hill." And Santa Fé took his hat off stylish and made the old lady the best sort of a bow.

Hill caught on quick and played right up to Santa Fé's lead. "That's our minister, Mr. Charles, ma'am. The one I've been telling you about," he said. "He's just friendly and sociable like that all the time. He looks after the folks in this town closer'n any preacher I ever knowed." A part of that, Hill said, was dead certain truth—seeing as Santa Fé had his eyes out straight

Santa Fé Charley's Kindergarten

along for everybody about the place who'd a dollar in his pocket, and wasn't satisfied till he'd scooped in that dollar over his table at the Forest Queen.

"There's the new church we're building," Hill went on, as they got to the top of the slope and headed for the deepo. "It ain't much to look at yet, the spire not being put on; and it won't show up well, even when it gets its spire on it, with churches East. But we're going to be satisfied with it, seeing it's the best we can do. You'll be interested to know, ma'am, your nephew give the land."

"William hasn't let on anything about it," Hart's aunt said, looking pleased all over. "But what in the world is a church doing with a railroad track running into it, Mr. Hill?"

Hill said he'd forgot about the track when he settled to use the new freight-house for church purposes; but he said he pulled himself together quick and told her the track was temp'ry — put in so building material could unload right on the ground. And then he took to talking about how obliging the railroad folks had been helping 'em—and kept a-talking that way till he got the coach to the deepo, and didn't need to hustle making things up any more. He said he never was so thankful in his life as he was when his stunt was done. He was just tired out, he said, lying straight ahead all day over thirty miles of bad road and not being able once to speak natural to his mules.

Hart was waiting at the deepo, on the chance his aunt would come in on the coach; and when she saw him she give a little squeal, she was so pleased, and hopped down in no time off the box—she was as brisk as a bee in her doings—and took to hugging him and half crying over him just like he was a little boy.

"Oh, William," she said, "I am *so* happy getting to you! And I'm happier'n I expected to be, finding out how quiet and respectable Palomitas is — not a bit what your letters made me think it was—and such real good people living in it, and everything but the queer country and the queer mud

houses just like it is at home. Mr. Hill has
been telling me all about it, coming over,
and about this new church you're building
that you gave the lot for. To think you've
never told me! Oh, William, I am so glad
and so thankful that out here in this wild
region you've kept serious-minded and are
turning out such a good man!"

Hart looked so mixed up over the way his
aunt was talking, and so sort of hopeless,
that Hill cut in quick and give him a lift.
"He's not much at blowing about himself,
your nephew ain't, ma'am," Hill said. "Why,
he not only give the land for the church over
there"—and Hill pointed at the freight-
house, so Hart could ketch on—"but it was
him got the Company to lay them temp'ry
tracks, so the building stuff could be took
right in. He's going to give a melodeon,
too."

"Dear William!" Hart's aunt said. "It
rejoices my heart you're doing all these
good deeds—and all the others Mr. Hill's
been telling me about. I must kiss you
again."

7   95

Santa Fé's Partner

"Oh, what I've done ain't nothing," Hart said, pulling himself together while she was kissing him. "Land's cheap, cheap as it can be, out here; and I give the Company such a lot of freight they're more'n willing to oblige me; and as to the melodeon—"

Hart sort of gagged when he got to the melodeon, and Santa Fé Charley — who'd come up while they all was talking away together—reached across the table and played his hand. "As to the melodeon, Mr. Hart," Santa Fé put in, "you said that being in business you could get it at a discount off. But that does not appreciably lessen your generosity, Mr. Hart; and your aunt"— Santa Fé took off his hat and bowed handsome—"is justified in taking pride in your good deeds. I am glad to tell her that in her nephew our struggling church has its stanchest pillar and its strongest stay."

"Yes, that's the way it is about the melodeon, Aunt Maria," Hart said, kind of weak and mournful. "Being in business, I get melodeons at such a discount off that giving 'em away ain't nothing to me at all.

Santa Fé Charley's Kindergarten

And now I guess we'd better be getting along home. It's a mighty mean home to take you to, Aunt Maria; but there's one comfort— as you'll find out when I get the chance to talk to you—you won't have to stay in it long."

There was a lot of the boys standing round on the deepo platform watching the show, and they all took their hats off respectful— following the lead Santa Fé give 'em—as Hart started away up the track, to where his store was, with his aunt on his arm. The town looked like some place East keeping Sunday: the Committee having talked strong as to what they'd do if things wasn't quiet, and having rounded up—and coralled in a back room Denver Jones lent the use of—the few who'd got drunk as usual because they had to, and so had to be took care of that way. It was a June evening, and the sun about setting; and somehow it all was so sort of peaceful and uncommon—with every-body in sight sober, and no fighting anywhere, and that little old lady going along, believing Palomitas was like that always, instead of

the hell on earth it was—some of us more'n
half believed we'd gone to sleep and got
stuck in a dream.

Things was made dreamier by the looks
and doings of the Sage-Brush Hen. She was
the only lady of the town, the Hen was, who
took part in the ceremonies—and likely it
was just about as well, for the sake of keeping
clear of surprises, the rest of 'em laid low.
As Hart and his aunt went off together up
the track, the Hen showed up coming along
down it; and she was dressed that pretty
and quiet—in the plainest sort of a white
frock, and wearing a white sun-bonnet—
and was looking so demure, like she could
when she'd a mind to, nobody knowed at
first who she was.

"Being the minister's wife, I've been taking the liberty, Mr. Hart," she said, smiling
pleasant, when the three of 'em come together on the track, "of looking around a
little up at your place to see that everything
has been fixed for your company the way it
should be." (She hadn't been nowheres near
Hart's place, it turned out — but Gospel

98

truth wasn't just what there was most of that day in Palomitas.) She went right on down the track without stopping, passing on Hart's side, and saying to him: "My husband expects you as usual at the Friendly Aid meeting to-morrow evening, Mr. Hart. We never seem half to get along, you know, when you're not there."

Hart's aunt give a little jump, and said: "Why, William, that must be Mrs. Charles, the minister's wife. What a pleasant-spoken lady she is! We met her husband just as we were driving into town."

Hart said he come pretty near saying back to her, "The hell you did!"—Hart talked that careless way, sometimes—but he said he pulled up before it got out, and all he did say was, "Oh!"

"She must be at the head of the Dorcas Society that Mr. Hill was telling me about," Hart's aunt went on; "and like enough she manages the kindergarten, too. I suppose, William, it's not surprising you haven't said anything in your letters about the Dorcas Society for all you were so liberal in helping

99

it—but I do think you might have told me about the kindergarten, knowing what a hobby of mine kindergartens are. I want to go and see it to-morrow morning, the first thing."

"It's—it's not in running order just now," Hart said. "Most of the children was took sick with the influenza last week, and there's whooping-cough and measles about, and so the school committee closed it down. And they had to stop, anyway, because they're going to put a new roof on. I guess it won't blow in again for about a month—or maybe more. In fact, I don't know—you see, it wasn't managed well, and got real down unpopular—if it 'll blow in again at all. I'm sorry you won't be able to get to it, Aunt Maria. Maybe it 'll be running if you happen to come out again next year."

"Why, how queer that is, William!" Hart's aunt said. "Mr. Hill told me it was the best kindergarten in New Mexico. But of course you know. Anyhow, I can see the school-room and the school fixtures, and Mrs. Charles can tell me about it when I go to the

Santa Fé Charley's Kindergarten

Dorcas Society—and that 'll do most as well. Of course I must get to the Dorcas Society. Mrs. Charles will take me, I'm sure. It meets, Mr. Hill says, every Thursday afternoon."

"Did he say where it was meeting now?" Hart asked. He was getting about desperate, he told Cherry afterwards; and what he wanted most was a chance to mash Hill's fool head for putting him in such a lot of holes.

"Of course he did, William," said Hart's aunt; "and I'm surprised you have to ask—seeing what an interest you take in the Society, and how you've helped it along. It was just lovely of you to give them all those goods out of your store to make up into clothes."

"That — that wasn't anything to do," Hart said. "What's in the store comes with a big discount—same as melodeons. Sometimes I feel as if I was saving money giving things away."

"You can talk about your generosity just as you please, William," she went on. "*I* think it's noble of you. And Mr. Hill said that Mrs. Major Rogers — who keeps the

Forest Queen Hotel, he said, and lets the
Society have a room to meet in for nothing—
said it was noble of you, too. I want to get
to know Mrs. Major Rogers right off. She
must be a very fine woman. She's an officer's
widow, Mr. Hill says, and a real lady, for all
she makes her living keeping a hotel out
here on the frontier. If she's a bit like that
sweet-looking Mrs. Charles I know we'll
get along. I'm surprised, William, you've
never told me what pleasant ladies live here.
It must make all the difference in the world.
Don't you think it would do for me not to be
formal, but just to go to Mrs. Major Rogers'
hotel to-morrow and call?"

"I guess—well, I guess you hadn't better
go right off the first thing in the morning,
Aunt Maria," Hart said. Thinking of his
aunt going calling at the Forest Queen and
running up against Tenderfoot Sal, he said,
gave him the regular cold shakes. "And
come to think of it," he said, "it's no use
your going to-morrow at all. Mrs.—Mrs.
Major Rogers, as I happen to know, went up
to Denver yesterday; and she won't be back,

she told me, before some time on in the end
of next week—likely as not, she said, she
wouldn't come then."

By that time they'd got along to Hart's
store, and Hart said: "Here's where I
live, Aunt Maria. You see what sort of a
place it is. But I've done my best to fix
things for you as well as I know how. Come
right along in—and when we've had supper
we've got to have a talk."

Along about ten o'clock that night Hart
come down to the Forest Queen looking pale
and haggard, and he was that broke up he
had to get three drinks in him before he
could say a word. Everybody was so interested, wanting to hear what he had to tell
'em, he didn't need to ask to have the game
stopped—it just stopped of its own accord.

When he'd had his third drink, and was
beginning to feel better, he said he couldn't
thank everybody enough for the way they'd
behaved; and that his aunt had gone to bed
tired out; and he'd been talking with her
steady for two hours getting things settled;

and she'd ended by agreeing she'd start back East with him the next night—he having made out he'd smash in his business if he waited a minute longer—and they was going by the Denver train. And he'd got her fixed he said, so she'd keep quiet through the morning—as she was going right at mending his stockings and things the first thing when she got up; and after that she was full of getting to work with canned peaches and making him a pie.

"But what's going to happen in the afternoon," he said, "the Lord only knows! That blasted fool of a Ben Hill"—Hart spoke just that bitter way about it—"hasn't had no more sense 'n to go and tell her this town's full of kindergartens, and she's so worked up there's no holding her, as kindergartens happens to be the fullest hand she holds. I've allowed we have one—things being as they was, I had to—but I've told her it's out of order, and the children laid up with whooping-cough, and the teacher sick a-bed, and the outfit damaged by a fire we had, and— and the Lord knows what I haven't told her

Santa Fé Charley's Kindergarten

about the damn thing." (Hart was that nervous he couldn't help speaking that way.) "But all I've said hasn't made no difference. She's just dead set on getting to what's left of that kindergarten, and I can't budge her. See it she will, she says; and I guess the up-shot of Hill's chuckle-headed talk 'll be to waste all the trouble we've took by landing us in the biggest give-away that ever was!" And Hart called for another drink, and had to set down to take it—looking pale.

All the boys felt terrible bad about the hole Hart was in; and they felt worse be-cause none of 'em hadn't no notion what a kindergarten did—when it did anything—and that made 'em more ashamed Palomitas hadn't one to show. Only Becker—Becker'd happened to come over from Santa Cruz that night—sized it up right; and Becker shook his head sort of dismal and said there wasn't no use even thinking about it — and that looked like a settler, because Becker seemed to know. Nobody didn't say nothing for a minute or two; and then Ike Williams spoke up—he was the boss carpenter on the freight-house job, Ike was—and said if what was wanted could be made out of boards, and made in a hurry, he'd lay off the freight-house gang the next morning and engage to have one ready by noon.

Santa Fé Charley'd been sitting still thinking, not saying a word. He let out a big cuss—and Charley wasn't given to cussing—when Ike made his offer; and then he banged his hand down on the table so hard he set the chips to flying, and he said: "Mr. Hart, don't you worry—we're going to put this job through!"

Everybody jumped up at that—some of 'em scrambling for the dropped chips—asking Santa Fé what he meant to do. But Charley wouldn't answer 'em. "Just you trust to Ike and me, Bill," he said. "We'll fix your kindergarten all right—only you keep on telling your aunt it ain't a good one, and how most of it got burned up in the fire. It's luck you let on to her there'd been a fire—that makes it as easy as rolling off a log. All you've got to do is to bring her down here at four o'clock to-morrow after-

Santa Fé Charley's Kindergarten

noon—you'd better till then keep her in the house, mending you up and making you all the pies she has a mind to—and when she gets here the kindergarten 'll be here, too!"

"Bring her here—to the Forest Queen?" Hart said, speaking doubtful.

"Bring her here—right here to the Forest Queen," Santa Fé said back to him. "You know pretty well I do things when I say I'll do 'em—and this thing 'll be done! Come to think of it," he said, "maybe it 'll be better if I go to your place and fetch her along myself. It 'll help if I do a little talking to her on the way down. Yes, we'll fix it that way. You and she be ready at four o'clock, and I'll come for you. That 'll give her an hour here, and an hour to go home and eat her supper—and that 'll get us to train-time, and then the circus 'll close down. Now you go home and go to bed, Bill. You're all beat out. Just you leave things to Ike and me and go right home."

Charley wouldn't say another word—so Hart had one more drink, for luck, and then he went home. He looked real relieved.

Santa Fé's Partner

When Santa Fé went to Hart's place, next afternoon, he had on his best black clothes, with a clean shirt and a fresh white tie; and he was that serious-looking you'd have sized him up for a sure-enough fire-escape anywhere on sight. Hart hadn't had no trouble, it turned out, keeping his aunt to home—she'd been working double tides ever since she got up, he said, making him things to eat and fussing over his clothes. They was all ready when Santa Fé come along, and the three of 'em stepped off down the track together—Hart having his aunt on his arm, and Santa Fé walking on ahead over the ties. Most of the boys was standing about watching the procession; but the girls—the Hen, likely, having told 'em to—was keeping on keeping quiet, and got what they could of it peeping through chinks in the windows and doors.

"Why, where *are* all the ladies, Mr. Charles?" Hart's aunt asked. "Except that sweet young wife of yours, it's just the mortal truth I haven't seen a single lady since I came into this town!"

Santa Fé Charley's Kindergarten

"They usually keep in-doors at this time of day, madam," Charley said. "They're attending to their domestic duties—and—and most of them, about now, are wont to be enjoying the tenderest happiness of mother-hood in nursing their little babes."

"It's very creditable they're such good housewives, I'm sure," said Hart's aunt; "only I do wish I could have met some of 'em and had a good dish of talk. But we'll be finding your wife at the kindergarten, I s'pose, and I'll have the pleasure of a talk with her. I've been looking forward all day to meeting her, Mr. Charles. She has one of the very sweetest faces I ever saw."

"I deeply regret to tell you, madam," said Santa Fé, "that my wife was called away suddenly last evening by a telegram. She had no choice in the matter. Her call was to minister to a sick relative in Denver, and of course she left immediately on the night train. Her disappointment at not meeting you was great. She had set her heart on showing you over our poor, half-ruined kin-dergarten—the fire did fearful damage—but her duty was too manifest to be ignored, and she had to leave that pleasant task to me."

"Now that is just too bad!" said Hart's aunt. "At least, Mr. Charles, I don't mean that exactly. It's very kind of you to take her place, and I'm delighted to have you. But I did so like your wife's looks, and I've been hoping she and I really'd have a chance to get to be friends."

That brought 'em to the Forest Queen, and Charley was more'n glad he was let out from making more excuses why his wife had shook her kindergarten job so sudden. "Here we are," he said. "But I must warn you again, madam, that our little kindergarten is only the ghost of what it was before the fire. We are hoping to get a new outfit shortly. On the very morning after the disaster a subscription was started—your nephew, as always, leading in the good work —and that afternoon we telegraphed East our order for fresh supplies. By the time that the epidemic of whooping-cough has abated—I am glad to say that all the children are doing well—we trust that our flock of little ones again can troop gladly to receive the elementary instruction that they delight in, and that my wife delights to impart."

"Why," said Hart's aunt, "the kindergarten's in Mrs. Major Rogers' hotel — the Forest Queen!"

"After the fire, Mrs. Major Rogers most kindly gave us the free use of one of her largest rooms," Santa Fé said; "and we are installed here until our own building can be repaired. I have spared you the sight, madam, of that melancholy ruin. I confess that when I look at it the tears come into my eyes."

"I don't wonder, I'm sure," said Hart's aunt. "I think I'd cry over it myself. But what a real down good woman Mrs. Major Rogers must be! Mr. Hill told me she gives the Dorcas Society the use of a room, too."

"She is a noble, high-toned lady, madam," Santa Fé said. "Since her cruel bereavement she has devoted to good works all the time that she can spare from the arduous duties by which she wins her livelihood. Words fail me say enough in her praise!

Santa Fé's Partner

Come right in, madam—but be prepared for a sad surprise!"

Hart said he didn't know how much surprised his aunt was—but he said when he got inside the Forest Queen, into the bar-room where Charley's faro layout usually was, he was so surprised himself he felt as if he'd been kicked by a mule!

There was the little tables for drinks, right enough; and out of the way in a corner with a cloth over it, same as usual, was the wheel. (It was used so little, the wheel was—nobody but Mexicans, now and then, caring for it—Santa Fé owned up afterwards he'd forgot it clean!) That much of the place was just as it always was; and the big table, taking up half the room, looked so natural—with the chairs up to it, and layouts of chips at all the places—that Hart was beginning to think Santa Fé was setting up a rig on him: 'till he seen what a lot of queer things besides chips there was on the table—and knowed they wasn't no game layout, and so sized 'em up to be what Charley'd scrambled together when he set out to play his kindergarten

Santa Fé Charley's Kindergarten

hand. And when he noticed the bar was curtained off by sheets he said he stopped worrying—feeling dead certain Charley'd dealt himself all the aces he needed to take him through.

"You don't need to be told, madam, being such an authority on kindergartens," said Santa Fé, "how inadequate is our little outfit for educational purposes. But you must remember that the fire destroyed almost everything, and that we have merely improvised what will serve our purposes until the new supply arrives. We succeeded in saving from the conflagration our large table, and our chairs, and most of the small tables— used by individual children having backward intellects and needing especial care. But nearly all of the other appliances of the school were lost to us, and damage was done to much of what we saved. Here, you see, is a little table with only three legs left, the fourth having been burned." And, sure enough, Hart said, Santa Fé turned up one of the little tables for drinks and one of its legs *was* burnt off! "All of our slates," he went ahead, "similarly were destroyed—and how much depends on slates in a kindergarten you know, madam, better than I do. Here is all that is left of one of them"—and he showed Hart's aunt a bit of burnt wood that looked like it had been part of a slate-frame afore it got afire.

"Dear me! Dear me!" said Hart's aunt. "It's just pitiful, Mr. Charles! I wonder how you can get along at all."

"It is not easy getting along, madam," Santa Fé said. "But we have managed to supply ourselves with a layout—I—that is—" I mean we have provided ourselves with some of the simpler articles of most importance; and with these, for the time being, we keep our little pupils' hands and minds not unprofitably employed. For instance, the ivory disks of various colors—which you see arranged upon the table as the pupils have left them—serve very successfully to elucidate the arithmetical processes of numeration, addition, and subtraction; and the more intelligent children are taught to observe that the disks of varying colors are

Santa Fé Charley's Kindergarten

varyingly numbered—white, 1; red, 5, and
blue, 10—and so are encouraged to identify
a concrete arbitrary figure with an abstract
thought."

"That's something new in kindergartening,
Mr. Charles," said Hart's aunt; "and it's as
good as it can be. I mean to put it right
into use in our kindergarten at home. Do
you get the disks at the places where they
sell kindergarten supplies?"

"Really, madam, I cannot tell you,"
Santa Fé said. "You see, we ordered what
would be needed through an agent East, and
these came along. I must warn you, however, that they are expensive."

Hart said, remembering what them chips
had cost him, one time and another, he
allowed to himself Charley was right and
they was about as expensive as they could
be!

"Our other little appliances, madam,"
Santa Fé went on, "are just our own make-
shift imitations of what you are familiar
with—building-blocks, and alphabet-blocks,
and dissected pictures, and that sort of

thing. Our local carpenter made the blocks for us, and we put on the lettering ourselves —as, indeed, its poor quality shows. The dissected pictures I am rather proud of, because Mrs. Charles may be said to have invented them.'' (It really was the Hen who'd made 'em, it turned out.) "The method is simple enough when you have thought of it, of course—and no doubt I value my wife's work unduly because I take so much pride in all that she does. You see, she just pasted pictures from the illustrated papers on boards; and then Mr. Williams— our carpenter, you know—sawed the boards into little pieces. And there you are!''

"Now that *was* bright of her!'' said Hart's aunt. "If you don't mind, I'll put one of the pictures together myself right now. I want to see how it looks, made that home-fashioned way.''

"I fear that our time is getting a little short, madam,'' said Santa Fé, in a hurry. "I've got my sermon to finish this afternoon, and I must be going in a few minutes now.'' The fact of the matter was he had to call her

off quick. It seems the Hen hadn't had anything but *Police Gazettes* to work on—and
while the bits looked all right jumbled up,
being put together they wouldn't have suited
nohow at all.

"Of course I mustn't keep you," said
Hart's aunt. "You've been more than kind,
Mr. Charles, to give me so much of your
valuable time as it is. I'm just like a child
myself, wanting to play with dissected pictures that way! But I must say that her
making them is a thing for your wife to be
proud of—and I hope you'll tell her so for
me."

"I guess we'd better be going now, Aunt
Maria," Hart said. "Mr. Charles has his
sermon to write, you know, and I want you
to have time to eat your supper comfortable
before we start down to the train."

"I do suppose we must go," said Hart's
aunt. "But I hate to, William, and that's
a fact! Just because it's so make-shifty,
this is the most interesting kindergarten I've
ever been in. When I get home I shall really
and truly enjoy telling the folks about it.

And I know how pleased they'll be, the same as I am, by finding what earnest-working men and women can do—out here in this rough country—with so little to go on but their wits and their own good hearts!"

And then she faced round sudden . on Santa Fé and said: "I see you have your table covered with green, Mr. Charles. What's that for? You've so many good notions about kindergartens that I'd like to know."

"Well, you see, madam, that green cover is a—it's a sort of—" Charley went slow for a minute, and then got a-hold of the card he wanted and put it down as smooth as you please. "That is an invention, madam," he said, "of my good wife's, too. Out here, where the sun is so violent, she said we must have a green cover on the table or the glare would be ruining all our dear little innocent children's eyes. And it has worked, madam, to a charm! Some of the children who had bad eyes to start with actually have got well!"

"Well, I do declare!" said Hart's aunt.

Santa Fé Charley's Kindergarten

"That wife of yours thinks so sensible she just beats all!"

Santa Fé give Hart a look as much as to say he'd got to get his aunt away somehow—seeing she was liable to break out a'most anywheres, and he'd stood about all he could stand. Hart allowed what Charley wanted was reasonable, and he just grabbed her by the arm and begun to lug her to the door. But she managed to give Santa Fé one more jolt, and a bad one, before she was gone.

"I haven't seen what this is," she said; and she broke off from Hart and went to where the wheel was standing covered up in the corner. "I s'pose I may look at it, Mr. Charles?" she said—and before either of 'em could get a-hold of her to stop her she had off the cloth. "For the land's sake!" she said. "Whatever part of a kindergarten have you got here?"

Hart said afterwards his heart went down into his boots, being sure they'd got to a give-away of the worst sort. Santa Fé said he felt that way for a minute himself; then he said he ciphered on it that Hart's aunt likely wouldn't know what she'd struck—and he braced up and went ahead on that chance.

"Ah," he said—speaking just as cool as if he was calling the deal right among friends at his own table—"that is one of the new German kindergarten appliances that even you, madam, may not have seen. We received it as a present from a rich German merchant in Pueblo, who was grieved by our pitiable plight and wanted to do what he could to help us after the fire."

"But what in the name of common-sense," said Hart's aunt, "do you do with it—with all those numbers around in circles, and that little ball?"

Charley had himself in good shape by that time, and he put down his words as sure as if they was aces—with more, if needed, up his sleeve. "It is used by our most advanced class in arithmetic, madam," he said. "The mechanism, you will observe, is arranged to revolve"—he set it agoing—"in such a way that the small sphere also is put in motion. And as the motion ceases"—it was slowing down to a stop—"the sphere

"'ONE OF THE NEW GERMAN KINDERGARTEN APPLIANCES'"

Santa Fé Charley's Kindergarten

comes to rest on one of the numbers painted
legibly on either a black or a red ground.
The children, seated around the table, are
provided with the numerating disks to which
I have already called your attention; and—
with a varying rapidity, regulated by their
individual intelligence — they severally, as
promptly as possible, arrange their disks in
piles corresponding with the number indicated by the purely fortuitous resting-place
of the sphere. The purpose of this ingenious
contrivance, as I scarcely need to point out
to you, is to combine the amusement of a
species of game with the mental stimulus
that the rapid computation of figures im-
parts. I may add that we arouse a desirable
spirit of emulation among our little ones by
providing that the child who first correctly
arranges his disks to represent the indicated
figure is given—until the game is concluded
—the disks of the children whose calculation
has been slow, or at fault."

"Well, of all things in the world, Mr.
Charles," said Hart's aunt, "to think of my
finding such a good thing as this out here

in New Mexico—when I've time and again
been over the best kindergarten-supply places
in Boston, and have been reading all I could
lay my hands on about kindergartens for
twenty years!"

"Oh, we do try not to be too primitive out
here, madam," said Santa Fé, taking a long
breath over having got through all right;
"and I am even vain enough to think that
perhaps we manage to keep pretty well up
with the times.   But I must say that it is a
pleasant surprise to me to find that I have
been able to give more than one point to a
lady like you, who knows every card—I
should say, to whom kindergarten processes
are so exceptionally well known.

"And now I really must beg your permission to leave you, that I may return to my
sermon.   I give much time to my sermons;
and I am cheered by the conviction—you
must not think me boastful—that it is time
well employed.   When I look around me and
perceive the lawless, and even outrageous,
conditions which obtain in so many other
towns in the Territory, and contrast them

Santa Fé Charley's Kindergarten

with the orderly rectitude of Palomitas, I
rejoice that my humble toil in the vineyard
has brought so rich a reward. I deeply regret, madam, that your present stay with us
must be so short; and with an equal earnest-
ness I hope that it may be my privilege soon
again to welcome you to our happy little
town."

Hart's aunt—she was just pleased all over
—was beginning to make a speech back to
him; but Santa Fé looked so wore out Hart
didn't give her the chance to go on. He just
grabbed her, and got her away in a hurry—
and Charley went to fussing with the cover
of the wheel, putting it on again, so she
couldn't get at him to shake hands for good-
bye. He said afterwards he felt that weak,
when he fairly was shut of her, all he could
do was to flop down into a chair anyway and
sing out to Blister Mike to come and get the
sheets off the bar quick and give him his
own bottle of Bourbon and a tumbler. And
he said he never took so many drinks,
one right on top of another, since he was
born!

Santa Fé's Partner

There was more'n the usual crowd down
at the deepo that night when the Denver
train pulled out—with Hart's aunt in the
Pullman, and Hart standing on the Pullman
platform telling the boys up to the last minute
how much he was obliged.

Things went that same Sunday-school way
right on to the end of the game; and Hart
said his aunt told him—as they was coming
along down to the deepo—she never would
a-believed there could be such a town as
Palomitas was, out in that wild frontier
country, if she hadn't seen it with her own
eyes. As to the ladies of the town, he said
she told him they certainly was the most
domestic she'd ever known!

Hart was so grateful—and he had a right
to be—he left a hunderd dollars with Tenderfoot Sal and told her to blow off the town
for him that night by running a free bar.
Sal done it, right enough—and that turned
out to be about the hottest night Palomitas
ever had. Most of the trouble was in the
dance-hall, where it was apt to be, and had
its start, as it did generally, right around the

Santa Fé Charley's Kindergarten

Sage-Brush Hen: who kept on being dressed up in her white frock and wearing her white sun-bonnet, and looked as demure as a cotton-tail rabbit, and cut up so reckless I reckon she about made a record for carryings on! Santa Fé had to fix one feller because of her —shooting him like he was used to, through his pants-pocket—and more'n a dozen got hurt in the ordinary way.

Some of the shooting didn't seem quite as if it was needed; but it was allowed after-wards—even if there hadn't been no free bar —there was excuse for it: seeing the town was all strung up and had to work itself off. Santa Fé, of course, had more excuse than anybody, being most strung-upest. Bluffing his way through that kindergarten game, he said, was the biggest strain he'd ever had. But he didn't mind what trouble he'd took, he said, seeing he'd got Hart out of his hole by taking it; and he looked real pleased when Hill spoke up—just about voicing what all the rest of us was thinking — saying he was ready, after the way he'd played his kindergarten hand, to put his pile on San-

Santa Fé's Partner

ta Fé Charley to make iced drinks in
hell!

Of course Hill oughtn't to have spoke like
that. But allowances was to be made for
Hill—owing to the ways he'd got into driving
mules.

V

AS I've said, folks in Palomitas mostly got for names what happened to come handiest and fitted. Likely that dude's cuffs was marked with something he was knowed by; but as most of us wasn't particular what his cuffs was marked, or him either, we just called him Boston— after the town he made out he belonged to— and let it go at that. Big game was what he said he was looking for: and Santa Fé Charley, with Shorty Smith and others helping, saw to it he got all he wanted and some over—but I reckon the exercises would a- been less spirited if the Sage-Brush Hen hadn't chipped in and played a full hand.

IIe was one of the sporting kind, Boston

was, that turned up frequent in the Territory in them days. Most of 'em was friends of officers at some of the posts, with a sprinkling throwed in of sons and nephews of directors of the road. Big game was what they all made out they come for; and they was apt to have about as much use for big game—when they happened to find any—as a cat has for two tails. But they seemed to enjoy letting off ca'tridges—and used to buy what skins was in the market to take home.

Boston turned out to be a nephew—nephews was apt to be worse'n sons for stuckupness—and he come in one morning in a private car hitched onto the Denver train. He had a colored man along to cook and clean his guns for him—he had more things to shoot with, and of more shapes and sizes, than you ever seen in one place outside of a gun-store—and he was dressed that nice in green corduroys, with new-fangled knives and hunting fixings hanging all over him like he was a Christmas-tree, he might have hired out for a show. He wasn't a bad set-up young feller; but with them green clothes on, and being clean shaved and wearing eye-glasses, he did look just about what he truly was.

Wood had a wire a director's nephew was coming—he was the agent, Wood was—and orders to side-track his car and see he was took care of; and of course Wood passed the word along to the rest of us what sort of a game was on. But he begged so hard, Wood did, the town would hold itself in—saying if rigs was put up on a director's nephew he was dead sure to lose his job—we all allowed we'd give the young feller a day or two to turn round in, anyway; and we promised Wood—who was liked—we'd let the critter get through his hunting picnic without putting up no rigs on him if he made any sort of a show of knowing how to behave. Howsomedever, he didn't—and things started up, and nobody but Boston himself to blame for it, that very first night over in the bar-room at the Forest Queen.

He had Wood in to supper with him in his car, Boston did, the darky cooking it; and

Santa Fé's Partner

Wood said—except it begun with their having pickled green plums, and some sort of messed-up stuff that tasted like spoilt salt fish and made him feel sickish—it was the best supper he ever eat. Each of 'em had a bottle of iced wine, he said; and he said they topped off with coffee that only wanted milk to make it a real wonder, and a drink like rock-and-rye, but chalks better, and such seegars as he'd never smoked in his born days.

All the time they was hashing—and Wood said he reckoned they was at it a'most a full hour—Boston kept a-telling what a hell of a one (that was the sort of careless way Wood put it) he was at big-game hunting; but Wood judged—taking all his talk together—the only thing he'd ever really shot bigger'n a duck or a pa'tridge was a deer the dogs had chased into a pond for him so it hadn't no chance. But it wasn't none of Wood's business to stop a director's nephew from blowing if he felt like it, and so he just let him fan away. Bears wasn't bad sport, he said, and he didn't mind filling in time with 'em if he couldn't get nothing better; but what he'd come to Palomitas for 'special, he said, was mountain-lions—he seemed to have it in his head he'd find 'em walking all over the place, same as cats—and he wanted to know if any'd lately been seen.

Wood told him them animals wasn't met with frequent in them parts (and they wasn't, for a fact, and hadn't been for about a hunderd years, likely) and maybe he'd do better to set his mind on jack-rabbits—which there was enough of out in the sage-brush, Wood told him, to load his car. And then he looked so real down disappointed, seeming to think jack-rabbits wasn't anyways satisfactory, Wood said he told him there was chances some of the boys over at the Forest Queen—they being all the time out in the mountains looking for prospects—might put him on to finding a bear, anyway; and it wouldn't do no harm to go across to the Queen and ask. And so over the both of 'em come.

It was Wood's mistake bringing that green-corduroyed pill right in among the boys with-

out giving notice, and Wood owned up it was
later—allowing he'd a-been more careful if
the rock-and-rye stuff on top of the wine, not
being used to either of 'em, hadn't loaded
him more'n he knowed about at the time.
Boston didn't seem to be much loaded, likely
having the habit of taking such drinks and
so being able to carry 'em; but he was that
high-horsey—putting on his eye-glasses and
staring 'round the place same as if he'd
struck a menagerie and the boys was beasts
in cages—all hands was set spiteful to him
right off.

Things was running about as usual at the
Queen: most of the boys setting around the
table and Santa Fé dealing; a few of 'em
standing back of the others looking on; two
or three getting drinks at the bar and talking to Blister; and the girls kicking their
heels on the benches, waiting till it come
time to start up dancing in the other room.
The only touch out of the common was the
way the Sage-Brush Hen had fixed herself—
she being rigged up in the same white duds
she'd wore when Hart's aunt come to town,

"STARING 'ROUND THE PLACE SAME AS IF HE'D STRUCK A
MENAGERIE"

and looking so real cute and pretty in 'em, and acting demure to suit, nobody'd ever a-sized her for the gay old licketty-split Hen she was.

It was between deals when Wood and Boston come in, and Santa Fé got up from the table and crossed over to 'em—Charley always was that polite you'd a-thought he was a fish-hook with pants on—and told Boston he hoped he seen him well, and was glad he'd come along. Then Wood told how he was after mountain-lions, and wasn't likely to get none; and Charley owned up they was few, and what there was of 'em was so sort of scattered the chances for finding 'em was poor.

Boston didn't say much of nothing at first, seeming to be took up with trying to make out where Santa Fé belonged to—hitching on his eye-glasses and looking him over careful, but only getting puzzleder the more he stared. You see, Charley—in them black clothes and a white tie on—looked for certain sure like he was a minister; and there he was getting up red-hot from dealing faro, and having on

each side of where he set at the table a forty-
five gun. It was more of a mix-up than
Boston could manage, and you could see he
didn't know where he was at. Howsomedever, Wood had told him he'd better make
out to be friendly, and take just what happened to come along without asking no
questions; and I reckon the shoat really
meant, as well as he knowed how to, to do
what he was told. So he give up trying to
size Santa Fé, and said back to him he was
obliged and was feeling hearty; and then he
took to grinning, like as if he wanted to
make things pleasant, and says: "Really, I
am very much interested in my surround-
ings. This place has quite the air of being a
barbarian Monte Carlo. It really has, you
know."

That was a non-plusser for Charley—and
Santa Fé wasn't non-plustered often, and
didn't like it when he was—but he pulled
himself together and put down what cards
he had: telling Boston monte was a game
he sometimes played with friends for amusement—which was the everlasting truth, only

the friends mostly was less amused than he was—and he'd had a dog named Carlo, he said, when he was a boy.

Boston seemed to think that was funny, and took to snickering sort of superior. He was about a full dose for uppishness, that young feller was: going on as if he'd bought the Territory, and as if the folks in it was the peones he'd took over—Mexican fashion—along with the land. Then he said he guessed Santa Fé did not ketch his meaning, and Monte Carlo was the biggest gambling hell there was.

Being in the business, Santa Fé was apt to get peevish when anybody took to talking about gambling; and Boston's throwing in hell on top of it that way was more'n he cared to stand. He didn't let on—at least not so the fool could see it—his dander was started, setting on himself being one of the things his work trained him to; but the boys noticed he begun to get palish up at the top of his forehead—where there was a white streak between his hair and where his hat come—and all hands knowed that for a bad sign. Boston, of course — being strangers with him—didn't know what Charley's signs was; and he just kept on a-talking as fresh as his green clothes.

"Not less psychologically than sociologically," says he, "is it interesting to find in this slum of the wilderness the degenerate Old-World vices in crude New-World garb. Here," says he, jerking his head across to the table," is a coarse reproduction of Monaco's essence; and there, I observe, are other repulsive features equally· coarse"—and he jerked his head over to where Shorty Smith was setting up drinks for Carrots at the bar.

"If you dare to say one word more about my features, young man," says Carrots—having a pug-nose, Carrots was techy about her features; and she had a temper the same color as her hair—"I'll smack you in the mouth!"

"And Oi'll smack your whole domn head off!" put in Blister Mike. "D'you think Oi'm going to have ladies drinking at my bar insulted by slush like you?" And Blister reached down to where he kept it among the tumblers to get his gun.

It looked as if there was going to be a ruction right off. There was Carrots red-hotter than her hair; and Blister, who was special friends with Carrots, shooting mad at having anybody sassing her; and Santa Fé's forehead getting whiter and whiter; and all hands on their hind legs at having Palomitas called a slum of the wilderness—and likely worse things said about the place in words nobody'd ever heard tell of longer'n your arm. The only one keeping quiet was Wood. He was sure, Wood was, trouble was coming beyond his stopping; and as he knowed which side his bread was buttered, and how he'd be fired from his job if things happened to go serious, he just went and sat down in a corner and swore to himself sorrowful, and was about the miserablest-looking man you ever seen alive. I guess it was more'n anything else being pitiful for Wood made things take the turn they did when the Sage - Brush Hen come into the game.

Santa Fé's Partner

"Now you all hear *me!*" the Hen sung out
sudden—and as the Hen wasn't much given
to no such public speaking, and the boys was
used to doing quick what she wanted when
she asked for it, everybody stopped talking
and Blister put his gun down on the bar.
Most of us, I reckon, had a feeling the Hen
was going to let things out in some queer
way she'd thought of in that funny head of
hers—same as she'd done other times when
matters was getting serious—and we all was
ready to help her with any skylarking she
was up to that would put a stop to the
rumpus and so get Wood out of his hole.
As for Boston—being too much of a fool to
know what he'd done to start such a racket—
he was all mazed-up by it: staring straight
ahead of him like a horse with staggers, and
looking like he wished he'd never been
born.

"You all hear *me*, I tell you!" says the
Hen, taking a-hold of Boston's arm sort of
motherly. "While I am the school-teacher
in Palomitas I shall not permit you boys to
play your pranks on strangers; and 'specially

138

not on this gentleman—whom I claim as a friend of mine because we both come from the same dear old town."

That was the first time anybody'd ever heard the Hen wasn't hatched-out in Kansas City. But it didn't seem as if calling her hand would be gentlemanly, so nobody said nothing; and off she went again—talking this time to Boston, but winking the eye away from him at the boys.

"It is merely a joke, sir," says the Hen, "that these young men are playing on you— and as silly a joke as silly can be. Sometimes, in spite of my most earnest efforts to stop them, they will go on in this foolish way: pretending to be wild and wicked and murderous and all such nonsense, when in reality there is not a single one among them who willingly would hurt a fly. What Miss Mortimer said about smacking you, as I hardly need to explain, was a joke too. Dear Miss Mortimer! She is as full of fun as a kitten, and as sweet and gentle"—Carrots, not seeing what the Hen was driving at, all the time was looking like a red-headed thunder-storm—"as the kindest-hearted kitten that ever was!

"And now, I assure you, sir, this reprehensible practical joking—for which I beg your indulgence—definitely is ended; and I am glad to promise that you will find in evidence, during the remainder of your stay in Palomitas, only the friendliness and the courtesy which truly are the essential characteristics of our seemingly turbulent little town."

The Hen stopped for a minute to get her wind back—which give the boys a chance to study over what they was told they was, and what kind of a town it turned out to be they was living in—and then off she went again, saying: "I beg that you will pardon me, sir, for addressing you so informally, without waiting for an introduction. We do not always stand strictly on etiquette here in Palomitas; and I saw that I had to put my cards down quick—I mean that I had to intervene hurriedly—to save you from being really annoyed. Now that I have cleared up the trifling misunderstanding, I trust satisfactorily, we will go back to where we ought to have started and I will ask Mr. Charles to introduce us." And round she cracked to Santa Fé and says: "Will you be so kind as to introduce my fellow-townsman to me, Mr. Charles?"

Santa Fé had begun to get a little cooled off by that time; and, like as not—it was a wonder the way them two passed cards to each other—the Hen give him some sort of a look that made him suspicion what her game was. Anyway, into it he come—saying to Boston, talking high-toned and polite like he knowed how to: "I have much pleasure, sir, in presenting you to Miss Sage, who is Palomitas's idol—and a near relative, as you may be interested in knowing, of the eminent Eastern capitalist of the same name. As she herself has mentioned, Miss Sage is our school-teacher; but her modest cheek would be suffused with blushes were I to tell you how much more she is to us—how broadly her generous nature prompts her to construe her duties as the instructress of innocent youth. Only a moment ago you had an

opportunity for observing that her word is
our law paramount. I am within bounds in
saying, sir, that in Palomitas she is univer-
sally adored."

"Oh, Mr. Charles! How can you!" says
the Hen, kind of turning away and looking
as if what Charley'd said really had made
her feel like blushing a little. Then she
faced round again and shook hands with
Boston—who was so rattled he seemed only
about half awake, and done it like a pump—
and says to him: "Mr. Charles is a born flat-
terer if ever there was one, sir, and you must
pay no attention whatever to his extrava-
gant words. I only try in my poor way, as
occasion presents itself"—she let her voice
drop down so it went sort of soft and ketchy
—"to mollify some of the harsher asperities
of our youthfully strenuous community; to
apply, as it were, the touchstone of Boston
social standards—the standards that you and
I, sir, recognize—to the sometimes too rough
ways of our rough little frontier settlement.
It is true, though, and I am proud to say it,
that the boys do like me — of course Mr.

Boston's Lion-hunt

Charles's talk about my being an idol and adored is only his nonsense; and it is true that they always are nice about doing what I ask them to do—as they were just now, when they were naughty and I had to make them behave.

"And now, since the formalities have been attended to and we have been introduced properly, and since you and I are fellow-Bostonians and ought to be friendly"—the Hen give him one of them fetching looks of hers—"you must come over to the bar and have a drink on me. And while we are performing this rite of hospitality," says the Hen—pretending not to see the jump he give —"we can discuss your projected lion-hunt: in which, with your permission, I shall take part." Boston give a bigger jump at that; and the Hen says on to him, sort of explaining matters: "You need not fear that I shall not sustain my end of the adventure. As any of the boys here will tell you, I can handle a forty-five or a Winchester about as well as anybody—and big-game hunting really is my forte. Indeed, I may say—using one of our

homely but expressive colloquialisms—that
when it comes to lion-hunting I am simply
hell!"

Boston seemed to be getting worse and
worse mixed while the Hen was rattling her
stuff off to him—and I reckon, all things con-
sidered, he wasn't to be blamed. He'd got
a jolt to start with, when he come in and
found what he took to be a preacher dealing
faro; and he was worse jolted when his fool-
talk—and he not knowing how he'd done it
—run him so close up against a shooting-
scrape. But the Hen was the limit: she
looking and acting like the school-ma'am she
said she was, and yet tangled up in a bar-
room with a lot of gamblers and such as
Kerosene Kate and old Tenderfoot Sal and
Carrots—and then bringing the two ends
together by talking one minute like he was
used to East, and the next one wanting to
set up drinks for him and telling him she
knowed all there was to know about gun-
handling and how at lion-hunting she was
just hell! I guess he was more'n half ex-
cusable, that young feller was, for looking

Boston's Lion-hunt

like he couldn't be counted on for telling for certain on which end of him was his heels!

What he did manage to work out clear in that fool head of his was he had the chance to get the drink he needed, and needed bad, to brace him; so over he come with the Hen to the bar and got it—and it seemed to do him some good. Then Carrots—who'd begun to ketch on a little to what the Hen was after—spoke up and told him it was true what Miss Sage had told him about her kittenishness, and she hadn't meant nothing when she was talking about smacking him; and to show he had no hard feeling, she said, he must have one on her. Then Blister Mike, having sized matters up, chipped in too: saying it would make him feel comfortabler—having done some joking himself by talking the way he did and getting his gun out—if they'd all have one on the bar.

As drinks in Palomitas was sighted for a thousand yards, and carried to kill further, by the time Boston had three of 'em in him—on top of the ones he'd had with Wood at supper—he was loaded enough to be careless about what was happening among the sun-spots and ready to take things pretty much as they come along. The boys was ready for what might be coming too: allowing for sure the Hen was getting a circus started, and only waiting to follow suit to the cards she put down.

What was needed, it turned out, was stacked with Shorty Smith; and the Hen sort of picked up Shorty with her eyes and says to him: "Your little boy Gustavus—he is *such* a dear little fellow, and I do love him so!—was telling me at recess to-day, Mr. Smith, that you saw a lion when you were out in the mountains day before yesterday prospecting. I think that very likely you may have seen the fierce creature even more recently; and perhaps you will have the kindness to tell us"—the Hen winked her off eye at Shorty to show him what was wanted—"where he probably may be found at the present time?"

Some of the boys couldn't help snickering right out when the Hen took to loading up Shorty with little Gustavuses; but Boston

Boston's Lion-hunt

didn't notice nothing, and Shorty—who had wits as sharp as pin-points, and could be counted on for what cards was needed in the kind of game the Hen was playing—put down the ace she asked for and never turned a hair.

"Gustavus will be tickled out of his little boots, Miss," says Shorty, "when I tell him how nice you've spoke about him; and I'm much obliged myself. He give it to you straight, the kid did, about that lion. I seen him, all right—and so close up it most scared the life out of me! And you're right, Miss, in thinking I've ketched onto him since— seeing I was a blame sight nearer to him than I wanted to be less'n four hours ago. Yes, ma'am, as I was coming in home to-night from the Cañada I struck that animal's tracks in the mud down by the ford back of the deepo—he'd been down to the river for a drink, I reckon—and they was so fresh he couldn't a-been more'n five minutes gone. When I got to thinking what likely might a-happened if I'd come along them five minutes sooner, Miss, I had cold creeps crawling all up and down the spine of my back!"

Santa Fé's Partner

Them statements of Shorty's set the boys
to snickering some more—there not being no
ford on the Rio Grande this side of La Chamita, and the wagon-bridge being down back
of the deepo where he said his ford was—but
Shorty paid no attention, and went on as
smooth as if he was speaking a piece he'd
got by heart.

"As you know, Miss, being such a hunter,"
says he—making up what happened to be
wanted about lions, same as he'd done about
fords—"them animals takes a drink every
four hours in the night-time as regular as if
they looked at their watches. Likely that
feller's bedded just a little way back in the
chaparral so's to be handy for his next one;
and I reckon if this sport here feels he needs
lions"—Shorty give his head a jerk over to
Boston—"he'll get one by looking for it right
now. But for the Lord's sake, Miss, don't
you think of taking a hand in tackling him!
He's a most a-terrible big one—the out and
out biggest I ever seen. The first thing you
knowed about it, he'd a-gulped you down
whole!"

Boston's Lion-hunt

"How you do go on, Mr. Smith!" says the Hen, laughing pleasant. "Have you so soon forgotten our hunt together last winter—when I came up and shot the grizzly in the ear just as he had you down and was beginning to claw you? And are you not ashamed of yourself, after that, to say that any lion is too big for me?"

Without stopping for Shorty to strain himself trying to remember that bear-hunt, round she cracked to Boston—giving Shorty and Santa Fé a chance to get in a corner and talk quick in a whisper—and says to him: "We just *are* in luck! These big old ones are the real fighters, you know. Only a year ago there was a gentleman from the East here on a lion-hunt—it was his first, and he did not seem to know quite how to manage matters—and one of these big fierce ones caught him and finished him. It was very horrible! The dreadful creature sprang on him in the dark and almost squeezed him to death, and then tore him to pieces while he still was alive enough to feel it, and ended by eating so much of him that only a few scraps of him were left to send East to his friends. This one seems to be just that kind. Isn't it splendid! What superb sport we shall have in getting him—you and I!"

What the Hen had to say about the way lions done business—'specially their eating hunters like they was sandwiches on a free-lunch counter—seemed to take some of the load off Boston, and as he got soberer he wasn't so careless as he'd been. From his looks it was judged he was thinking a lion some sizes smaller would be a better fit for him; but he couldn't well say so—with the Hen going on about wanting hers as big as they made 'em—so he took a brace, and sort of swelled himself out, and said the bigger this one was the better he'd be pleased.

"But I cannot permit you, my dear young lady," he says, "to share with me the great danger incident to pursuing so ferocious a creature. I alone must deal with it. To-morrow I shall familiarize myself with the locality where Mr. Smith has found its tracks; and to-morrow night, or the night after—as the weather may determine. Of course noth-

ing can be done in case of rain—I will seek
the savage brute in its lair. And then we
shall find out"—Boston worked up as much
as he could of a grin, but it seemed to come
hard and didn't fit well—"which of us shall
have the other's skin!"

"Danger for me!" says the Hen, giving
him another of them looks of hers. "Just
as though I would not be as safe, with a brave
man like you to protect me, as I am teaching
school! And to-morrow night, indeed! Do
you think lions are like dentists—only the
other way round about the teeth!" and the
Hen laughed hearty—"and you can make
appointments with them a week ahead!
Why, we must be off, you and I, this very
minute! I'll run right round home and get
my rifle—and meet you at your car as soon
as you've got yours. To think of our having
a lion this way almost sitting on the front-
door step! It's a chance that won't come
again in a thousand years!"

Away the Hen went a-kiting; and, there
not being no hole he could see to crawl out
of, away went Boston—only the schedule he

run on was some miles less to the hour. To make sure he didn't try to side-track, Shorty went with him — leaving Santa Fé to fix matters with the Hen, and do what talking was needed to ring in the boys.

Shorty put through his part in good shape: helping Boston get as many of his guns as he thought was wanted to hunt lions with— which was as many as he could pack along with him—and managing sort of casual to slip out the ca'tridges so he wouldn't hurt nobody. It turned out Shorty needn't a-been so extry-precautious—but of course he couldn't tell. By the time Shorty had him ready, the Hen come a-hustling up—having finished settling things with Santa Fé—and sung out to him to get a move on, or likely the lion would a-had his drink and gone. The move he got wasn't much of a one; but he did come a - creeping out of the car at last, and having such a load of weepons on him as give him some excuse for going slow.

"Good luck to you!" says Shorty, and off he skipped in a hurry to get at the rest of his

part of the ceremonies—not paying no attention to Boston's most getting down on his
knees to him begging him to come along.
Then Boston wanted the colored man to come
—who was scared out of his black skin at the
notion, and wouldn't; and if the Hen hadn't
ended up by grabbing a-hold of him—saying
as it was dark, and she knowed the way and
he didn't, she'd better lead him—likely she
wouldn't a-got him started at all. Pulling
him was more like what she did than leading
him, the Hen said afterwards; but she didn't
kick about his going slow and wanting to
stop every minute, she said, because it give
Santa Fé and Shorty more time.

The night was the kind that's usual in New
Mexico, and just what was wanted. There
was no moon, and the starshine — all the
stars looked to be about the size of cheeses—
give a hazy sort of light that made everything seem twice as big as it really was, and
shadows so black and solid you'd think you
could cut 'em in slices same as pies. And
it was so still you could a-heard a mouse
sneezing half a mile off. The rattling all

over him of Boston's weepons sounded like
there was boilers getting rivetted close by.

The Hen yanked him along easy, but kept
him a-moving—and passed the time for him
by telling all she could make up about what
desprit critters lions was. Starting from
where his car was side-tracked, they went
round the deepo; and then down the wagon-
road pretty near to the bridge, but not so
near he could see it; and then across through
the sage-brush and clumps of mesquite till
they come to the river—where there was a
break in the bluff, and a flat place going on
down into the water that looked like it was
the beginning of a ford. For a fact, it was
where the Mexican women come to do their
clothes-washing, and just back from the
river was a little 'dobe house—flat-topped,
and the size and shape of a twelve-foot-
square dry-goods box — the women kept
their washing things in. But them was par-
ticulars the Hen didn't happen to mention to
Boston at the time.

When they come to the 'dobe she give him
a jerk, to show him he was to stand still there;

Boston's Lion-hunt

and then she grabbed him close up to her, so she could whisper, and says: "It was here that Mr. Smith saw the ferocious animal's foot-marks almost precisely four hours ago. The habits of these creatures are so regular, as Mr. Smith mentioned, that this one certainly will return for his next drink when the four hours are ended — and so may be upon us at any moment. I hope that we may see him coming. If he saw us before we saw him — well, it wouldn't be nice at all!"

The Hen let that soak in a little; and then she snuggled up to Boston, all sort of shivery, and says: "I wish that we had taken the precaution to ask Mr. Smith from which direction the tracks came. These lions, you know, have a dreadful way of stealing up close to you and then springing! That was what happened to that poor young man. So far as was known, his first notice of his peril was finding himself crushed to the ground beneath the creature's weight—and the next instant it was tearing him with its teeth and claws. I — I begin to wish I hadn't come!" And the Hen snuggled up closer and shivered bad.

Boston seemed to be doing some shivers on his own account, judging from the way his guns rattled; and his teeth was so chattery his talking come queer. But he managed to get out that if they was inside the house they'd have more chances—and he went to work trying to open the door. When he found he couldn't—it being locked so good there was no budging it—he got worse jolted, and his breath seemed to be coming hard.

The Hen got a-hold of him again and done some more shivers, and then she says: "It all will be over, one way or the other, in a very few moments now. And oh, how thankful I am—since so needlessly and so foolishly I have placed myself in this deadly peril—that I have for my protector a brave man! If salvation is possible, you will save me I am sure!"

Boston tried to say something, but he'd got so he was beyond talking and only gagged; and while he was a-gagging there come a queer noise—sounding like it was a critter

Boston's Lion-hunt

crawling around in among the bushes—that
made him most jump out of his skin! Down
went his guns on the ground all in a clatter;
and he was scared so limp he'd a-gone down
a-top of 'em if the Hen hadn't got a good grip
on him with both arms. They stood that
way more'n a minute, with him a-shaking all
over and the Hen doing some shaking for
company—and then she hiked him round so
he pointed right and says: "Look! Look!
There by those little bushes! Oh how horrible!" And the Hen give a groan.

What was wanted to be looked at was on
hand, right enough—and I reckon it showed
to most advantage by about as much light as
it got from the stars. All they could make
sure of was something alive, moving sort of
awkward and jumpy, coming out from a
tangle of mesquite bushes not more'n three
rods off and heading straight for 'em; and
seeing it the way they did — just a black
splotch all mixed in with the shadows of the
bushes—it looked to be most as big as a cow!
Limp as he was—so you'd a-thought there
wasn't any yell in him—Boston let off a yell

that likely was heard clear across the mesa
at San Juan!

"Shoot!" says the Hen. "I can't. I'm
too frightened. Shoot quick — or we are
lost!" She let go of him, so he could reach
down to where he'd spilled his gun-shop and
get a weepon; but Boston wasn't on the shoot,
and he hadn't no use for weepons just then.
All he wanted to do was to run; and if the
Hen hadn't got a fresh grip on him and held
him—she was a strapping strong woman, the
Hen was—he would a-made a bolt for it
certain sure.

"No! No! Don't attempt to run!" says
the Hen, talking scared and desprit. "In
an instant, should we turn our backs on him,
the terrible creature would be upon us with
one long cruel bound!"

From the way the terrible creature, as the
Hen called him, was a-going on — sort of
hopping up and down, and not making much
headway—it didn't look as if long cruel
bounds was what he was most used to. But
Boston wasn't studying the matter extra
careful, and as the Hen found he took pretty

much what she give him she just cracked along.

"To run, I tell you," says the Hen, "is but to court the quicker coming of the torturing death to which we are doomed. It will come quick enough, anyway!"—and she handed out a fresh lot of shivers, and throwed in sobs. Then she give a jump, as if the notion 'd just struck her, and says: "There *is* a chance for us! Up on the roof of this house we may be safe. Lions can spring enormous distances horizontally, you know; but, save in exceptional cases, their vertical jumping powers are restricted to a marked degree. Quick! Put your foot in my hand and let me start you. When you are up, you can pull me up after you. Now then!"—and the Hen reached her hand down so she could get a-hold of Boston's foot and give him a send.

Her using them long words about the way lions did their jumping—being the kind of talk he was used to—seemed to sort of brace him. Anyways—the lion helping hurry things by just then giving another jump or two—

he managed to have sense enough to put his foot in the Hen's hand, same as she told him; and then she let out her muscle and give him such an up-start he was landed on the roof of the 'dobe afore he fairly knowed he'd begun to go! Being landed, he just sprawled out flat—and getting the Hen up after him seemed to be about the last thing he had on his mind.

"Help! Help!" sung out the Hen. "The lion is almost on me! Give me your hand!" But Boston wasn't in no shape to give hands to nobody. All he did was to kick his legs about and let off groans.

"Oh, I understand, now," says the Hen in a minute. "You are crying out in the hope of luring the creature into trying to reach you—as he can, if he happens to be one of the exceptional jumpers—and so give me a chance to get away. How noble that is of you! I shall take the chance, my brave preserver, that your self-sacrifice gives me— and I shall collect, and bedew with tears of gratitude, all that the savage monster leaves me of your bones! Heaven bless you—and

Boston's Lion-hunt

good-bye!'' And away the Hen cut—leaving
Boston high and dry on the roof of the 'dobe,
so scared he just lay there like a wet rag.

She didn't cut far, the Hen didn't. The
rest of us was a-setting around under the
mesquite bushes, and she joined the party
and set down too—stuffing her handkerchief
into her mouth, and holding both hands
jammed tight over it, to keep from yelling
out with the laugh that was pretty near
cracking her sides.

Then we all waited till daylight—with
Shorty, who had charge of the lion, working
that animal as seemed to be needed whenever
Boston quieted down with his groans. All
hands really enjoyed theirselves, and it was
one of the shortest nights I think I ever
knowed.

Daylight comes sudden in them parts.
One minute it's so darkish you can't see nothing—and the next minute the sun comes up
with a bounce from behind the mountains
and things is all clear.

When the sun did his part of the work and

give all the light was needed, we done ours—which was coming out from among the mesquite bushes and saying good-morning polite to Boston, up on the roof of the 'dobe, and then taking the hobbles off old man Gutierrez's jackass so it could walk away home.

The Hen felt she needed to have one more shot, and she took it. "My brave preserver!" says the Hen, speaking cheerful. "Come down to me—that I may bedew with tears of gratitude your bones!"

VI

OME of them summer days in Palomitas was that hot they'd melt the stuffing out of a lightning-rod, and you could cook eggs in the pockets of your pants. When things was that way the town was apt to get quieted down — most being satisfied to take enough drinks early to make it pleasant spending the rest of the day sleeping 'em off somewheres in the shade. Along late in the afternoon, though, the wind always breezed down real cool and pleasant from the mountains — and then the boys would wake up and get a brace on, and whatever was going to happen would begin.

Being that sort of weather, nobody was paying no attention worth speaking of to

163

nothing: and when the Denver train come in—being about three hours late, like it had a way of being, after a wash-out—the place was in such a blister that pretty much all you could hear to show anybody was alive in Palomitas was snores. Besides Wood—who had to be awake to do his work when the train got there—and the clump of Mexicans that always hung around the deepo at train-time, there wasn't half a dozen folks with their eyes open in the whole town.

Santa Fé Charley was one of the few that was awake and sober. He made a point, Santa Fé did, of being on hand when the train come in because there always was chances somebody might be aboard he could do business with; and he had to keep sober, mostly, same as I've said, or he couldn't a-done his work so it would pay. He used to square things up—when he really couldn't stand the strain no longer—by knocking off dealing and having a good one lasting about a week at a time. It was while he was on one of them tears of his, going it worse'n usual, he got cleaned out in Denver Jones's

Shorty Smith's Hanging

place—and him able, when he hadn't a jag on, to wipe up the floor with Denver!—and then went ahead the next day, being still jagged, and shot poor old Bill Hart. But them is matters that happened a little later, and will be spoke of further on.

When the train pulled in alongside the deepo platform it didn't seem at first there was nobody on it but the usual raft of Mexicans with bundles in the day-coach—who all come a-trooping out, cluttered up with their queer duds, and went to hugging their aunts and uncles who was waiting for 'em in real Mexican style. Charley looked the lot over and seen there was nothing in it worth taking time to; and then he got his Denver paper from the messenger in the express-car and started off to go on back to his room in the Forest Queen.

Down he come along the platform—he was a-looking at his *Tribune*, and not paying no attention—and just as he got alongside the Pullman a man stepped off it and most plumped into him; and would a-plumped if he hadn't been so beat out by the hot weather he was going slow. He was a little round friendly looking feller, with a red face and little gray side-whiskers; and he was dressed up in black same as Charley was—only he'd · a shorter-tailed coat, and hadn't a white tie on, and was wearing a shiny plug hat that looked most extra unsuitable in them parts on that sort of a day.

"I beg your pardon, sir!" says the little man, as he pulled himself up just in time to keep from bumping.

Charley bowed handsome—there was no ketching off Santa Fé when it come to slinging good manners, his being that gentlemanly he could a-give points to a New York barkeep—and says back: "Sir, I beg yours! Heedlessness is my besetting sin. The fault is mine!" And then he said, keeping on talking the toney way he knowed how to: "I trust, sir, that you are not incommoded by the heat. Even for New Mexico in August, this is a phenomenally hot day."

"Incommoded is no name for it!" says the little man, taking off his shiny hat and mop-

"'IT'S HOTTER THAN SAHARA!' SAID THE ENGLISHMAN"

Shorty Smith's Hanging

ping away at himself with his pocket-hand-kerchief. "I've never encountered such heat anywhere. It's hotter than Sahara! In England we have nothing like it at all." Then he mopped himself some more, and went ahead again — seeming glad to have somebody to let out to: "My whole life long I've been finding fault with our August weather in London. I'll never find fault with it again. I'd give fifty pounds to be back there now, even in my office in the City—and I'd give a hundred willingly if I could walk out of this frying-pan into my own home in the Avenue Road! If you know London, sir, you know that St. John's Wood is the coolest part of it, and that the coolest part of St. John's Wood—up by the side of Primrose Hill—is the Avenue Road; and so you can understand why thinking about coming out from the Underground and walking homeward in the cool of the evening almost gives me a pain!"

Santa Fé allowed he wasn't acquainted with that locality; but he said he hadn't no doubt—since you couldn't get a worse one—

it was a better place in summer than Palomitas. And then he kind of chucked it in casual that as the little man didn't seem to take much stock in Palomitas maybe he'd a-done as well if he'd stuck at home.

Charley's talking that way brought out he wasn't there because he wanted to be, but because he was sent: coming to look things over for the English stockholders—who was about sick, he said, of dropping assessments in the slot and nothing coming out when they pushed the button—before they chipped in the fresh stake they was asked for to help along with the building of the road. He said he about allowed, though, the call was a square one, what he'd seen being in the road's favor and as much as was claimed for it; but when it come to the country and the people, he said, there was no denying they both was as beastly as they could be. Then he turned round sudden on Santa Fé and says: "I infer from your dress, sir, that you are in Orders; and I therefore assume, that you represent what little respectability this town has. Will you kindly tell me if it is possible in this filthy place to procure a brandy-and-soda, and a bath, and any sort of decent food?"

It always sort of tickled Santa Fé, same as I've said, when a tenderfoot took him for a fire-escape; and when it happened that way he give it back to 'em in right-enough parson talk. So he says to the little man, speaking benevolent: "In our poor way, sir, we can satisfy your requirements. At the Forest Queen Hotel, over there, you can procure the liquid refreshment that you name; and also food as good as our little community affords. As for your bath, we can provide it on a scale of truly American magnificence. We can offer you a tub, sir, very nearly two thousand miles long!"

"A tub two thousand miles long?" says the little man. "Oh, come now, you're chaffing me. There can't be a tub like that, you know. There really can't!"

"I refer, sir," says Santa Fé, "to the Rio Grande."

The little man took his time getting there, but when he did ketch up he laughed hearty. "How American that is!" says he. And

then he says over again: "How American
that is!"—and he laughed some more. Then
he said he'd start 'em to getting his grub
ready while he was bathing in that two-
thousand-mile bath-tub, and he'd have his
brandy-and-soda right away; and he asked
Charley—speaking doubtful, and looking at
his white necktie—if he'd have one too?

Charley said he just would; and it was
seeing how sort of surprised the little man
looked, he told the boys afterwards, set him
to thinking he might as well kill time that hot
day trying how much stuffing that sort of a
tenderfoot would hold. He said at first he
only meant to play a short lone hand for the
fun of the thing; and it was the way the little
man swallowed whatever was give him, he
said, that made the game keep on a-growing
—till it ended up by roping in the whole
town. So off he went, explaining fatherly
how it come that preachers and brandys-and-
sodas in Palomitas got along together first
class.

"In this wildly lawless and sinful community, sir," says he, "I find that my humble

Shorty Smith's Hanging

efforts at moral improvement are best advanced by identifying my life as closely as may be with the lives of those whom I would lead to higher planes. At first, in my ignorance, I held aloof from participating in the customs — many of them, seemingly, objectionable — of my parishioners. Naturally, in turn, they held aloof from me. I made no impression upon them. The good seed that I scattered freely fell upon barren ground. Now, as the result of experience, and of much soulful thought, I am wiser. Over a friendly glass at the bar of the Forest Queen, or at other of the various bars in our little town, I can talk to a parishioner with a kindly familiarity that brings him close to me. By taking part in the games of chance which form the main amusement of my flock, I still more closely can identify their interests with my own—and even materially improve, by such winnings as come to me in our friendly encounters, our meagre parish finances. I have as yet taken no share in the gun-fights which too frequently occur in our somewhat tempestuous little community; but I am

Santa Fé's Partner

seriously considering the advisability of still farther strengthening my hold upon the respect and the affection of my parishioners by now and then exchanging shots with them. I am confident that such energetic action on my part will tend still more to endear me to them—and, after all, I must not be too nicely fastidious as to means if I would compass my end of winning their trust and their esteem."

While Santa Fé was talking along so slick about the way he managed his parsoning, the little man's eyes was getting bulgier and bulgier; and when it come to his taking a hand in shooting-scrapes they looked like they was going to jump out of his head. All he could say was: "Good Lord!" Then he kind of gagged, and said he'd be obliged if he could get his brandy-and-soda right off.

Charley steered him across to the Forest Queen, and when he had his drink in him, and another on top of it, he seemed to get some of his grip back. But even after his drinks he seemed like he thought he must be asleep and dreaming; and he said twice over

Shorty Smith's Hanging

he'd never heard tell of such doings in all his born days.

Santa Fé just give a wink across the bar to Blister Mike—who didn't need much winking, being a wide-awake one—and then he went ahead with some more of the same kind. "No doubt, my dear sir, in the older civilization to which you are accustomed my methods would seem irregular — perhaps even reprehensible. In England, very likely, unfavorable comment would be made upon a pastor who cordially drank with members of his flock at public bars; who also—I do not hesitate, you see, to give our little games of chance their harshest name — in a friendly way gambled with them; and I can imagine that the spectacle of a parish priest engaging with his parishioners, up and down the street of a quiet village, in a fight with six-shooters and Winchesters would be very generally disapproved."

"It is impossible, quite impossible," says the little man, sort of gaspy, "to imagine such a horrible monstrosity!"

"Very likely for you, sir," says Charley,

173

speaking affable, "it is. But you must remember that ours is a young and a vigorous
community—too young, too vigorous, to be
cramped and trammelled by obsolete con-
ventions and narrow Old-World rules. Life
with us, you see, has an uncertain suddenness
—owing to our energetic habit of settling our
little differences promptly, and in a decisive
way. At the last meeting of our Sunshine
Club, for instance—as the result of a short
but heated argument—Brother Michael, here,
felt called upon to shoot a fellow-member.
While recognizing that the occurrence was
unavoidable, we regretted it keenly—Brother
Michael most of all."

"Sure I did that," said Blister, playing out
quick to the lead Charley give him. "But
your Reverence remembers he drew on me
first—and if he'd been sober enough to shoot
straight it's meself, and not him, would be
by now living out in the cemetery on the
mesa; and another'd be serving your drinks
to you across this bar. I had the rights on
my side."

"Precisely," says Charley. "You see, sir,

Shorty Smith's Hanging

it was a perfectly fair fight. Brother Michael and his fellow-member exchanged their shots in an honorable manner — and, while we mourn the sudden decease of our friend lost to us, our friend who survives has suffered no diminution of our affectionate regard. Had the shooting been unfair, then the case would have gone into another category—and our community promptly would have manifested the sturdy sense of justice that is inherent in it by hanging the man by whom the unfair shot had been fired. Believe me, sir"—and Santa Fé stood up straight and stuck his chest out—"Palomitas has its own high standards of morality: and it never fails to maintain those standards in its own stern way!"

The little man didn't say nothing back. He looked like he was sort of mazed. All he did was to ask for another brandy-and-soda; and when he'd took it he allowed he'd skip having his bath and get at his eating right away—saying he was feeling faintish, and maybe what he needed was food. Of course that was no time of day to get victuals: but

Santa Fé's Partner

Santa Fé was a good one at managing, and he fixed it up so he had some sort of a hash layout; and before he went at it he give him a wash-up in his own room.

It was while he was hashing, Charley said, the notion come to him how Palomitas might have some real sport with him—the same kind they had when Hart's aunt come on her visit, only twisting things round so it would be the holy terror side of the town that had the show. And he said as he'd started in with the preacher racket, he thought they might keep that up too—and make such an out and out mix-up for the little man as would give cards to any tenderfoot game that ever was played. Santa Fé always was full of his pranks: and this one looked to pan out so well, and was so easy done, that he went right across to the deepo and had a talk with Wood about how things had better be managed; and Wood, who liked fun as much as anybody, caught on quick and agreed to take a hand.

The little man seemed to get a brace when he had his grub inside of him; and over he

Shorty Smith's Hanging

went to the deepo and give Wood the order
he had from the President to see the books—
and was real intelligent, Wood said, in finding
out how railroading in them parts was done.
But when he'd cleaned up his railroad job,
and took to asking questions about the
Territory, and Palomitas, and things generally—and got the sort of answers Santa
Fé had fixed should be give him, with some
more throwed in—Wood said his feet showed
to be that tender he allowed it would a-hurt
him with thick boots on to walk on boiled
beans.

Wood said he guessed he broke the lying
record that afternoon; and he said he reckoned if the little man swallowed half of what was
give him, and there wasn't much of anything
he gagged at, he must a-thought Palomitas—
with its church twice Sundays and prayer-
meetings regular three times a week, and its
faro-bank with the preacher for dealer, and
its Sunshine Club that was all mixed in with
shooting-scrapes, and its Friendly Aid Society
that attended mostly to what lynchings was
needed—was something like a bit of heaven

that had broke out from the corral it belonged in and gone to grazing in hell's front yard!

When he'd stuffed him as much as was needed, Wood told him—Santa Fé having fixed it that way—there was a Mexican church about a thousand years old over in the Cañada that was worth looking at; and he told him he'd take him across on his buckboard to see it if he cared to go. He bit at that, just as Santa Fé counted on; and about four o'clock off they went—it was only three mile or so down to the Cañada—in good time to get him back and give him what more was coming to him before he started off North again on the night train. Wood said the ride was real enjoyable—the little man showing up as sensible as anybody when he got to the church and struck things he knowed about; and it turned out he could talk French, and that pleased the padre—he was that French one I've spoke about, who was as white as they make 'em—and so things went along well.

The wind had set in to blow down the valley cool and pleasant as they was getting

Shorty Smith's Hanging

along home; and coming down on it, when
they got about half a mile from Palomitas,
they begun to hear shooting—and it kept on,
and more of it, the closer they come to town.
Knowing what Santa Fé had set the boys up
to, Wood said he pretty near laughed out
when he heard it; but he held in, he said—
and told the little man, when he asked what
it meant, that it didn't mean nothing in particular: being only some sort of a shooting-
scrape, like enough—the same as often happened along about that time in the afternoon.

He said the little man looked queerish,
and wanted to know if the men in the town
was shooting at a target; and when Wood said
he guessed they was targetting at each other,
and likely there'd be some occurrences, he
said he looked queerisher — and said such
savagery was too horrible to be true. But
he wasn't worried a bit about himself, Wood
said—he was as nervy a little man, Wood
said, as he'd ever got up to—and all he wanted was to have Wood whip the mules up,
so he'd get there quick and see what was
going on. Wood whipped up, right enough,

and the mules took 'em a-kiting—going at a full run the last half-mile or so, and not coming down to a walk till they'd crossed the bridge over the Rio Grande and was most to the top of the hill. At the top of the hill they stopped—and that was a good place to stop at, for the circus was agoing on right there.

Things really did look serious; and Wood said—for all he'd been told what was coming —he more'n half thought the boys had got to rumpussing in dead earnest. Three or four was setting on the ground with their sleeves and pants rolled up tying up their arms and legs with their pocket-handkerchiefs; there was a feller—Nosey Green, it turned out to be —laying on one side in a sort of mixed-up heap like as if he'd dropped sudden; right in the middle of the road Blister Mike was sprawled out, with Santa Fé—his black clothes all over dust and his hat off—holding his head with one hand and feeling at his heart with the other; and just as the buckboard stopped, right in the thick of it, Kerosene Kate come a-tearing along, with the

Shorty Smith's Hanging

Sage-Brush Hen close after her, and plumped down on Mike and yelled out: "Oh, my husband! My poor husband! He is foully slain!"

It was all so natural, Wood said, that seeing it sudden that way give him a first-class jolt. For a minute, he said, he couldn't help thinking it was the real thing. As for the little man—and he likely would have took matters just the same, and no blame to him, if his feet had been as hard as anybody's —he swallowed the show whole. "Good Heavens!" says he, getting real palish. "What a dreadful thing this is!"

Santa let go of Mike's head and got up, brushing his pants off, and says solemn: "Our poor brother has passed from us. Palomitas has lost one of its most useful citizens—there was nobody who could mix drinks as he could—and the world has lost a noble man! Take away his stricken wife, my dear," he says, speaking to the Sage-Brush Hen. "Take poor Sister Rebecca home with you to the parsonage—my duties lie elsewhere at present—and pour out to her from your tender heart the balm of comfort that you so well know how to give."

Then he come along to the buck-board, and says to the little man: "I greatly regret that this unfortunate incident should have occurred while you are with us. From every point of view the event is lamentable. Brother Green, known familiarly among us because of his facial peculiarity as Nosey Green—the gentleman piled up over there on the other side of the road—was as noble-hearted a man as ever lived; so was Brother Michael, whom you met in all the pride of his manly strength only this morning at the Forest Queen bar. Both were corner-stones of our Sunshine Club, and among the most faithful of my parishioners. In deep despondency we mourn their loss!"

"It is dreadful—dreadful!" says the little man. And then he wanted to know how the shooting begun.

"The dispute that has come to this doubly fatal ending," says Santa Fé, shaking his head sorrowful, "related to cock-tails. In what I am persuaded was a purely jesting

Shorty Smith's Hanging

spirit, Brother Green cast aspersions upon
Brother Michael's skill as a drink-mixer. The
injustice of his remarks, even in jest, aroused
Brother Michael's hot Celtic nature and led
to a retort, harshly personal, that excited
Brother Green's anger—and from words they
passed quickly to a settlement of the matter
with their guns. However, as the fight was
conducted by both of them in an honorable
manner, and was creditable equally to their
courage and to their proficiency in the use
of arms, it is now a back number and we may
discharge it from our minds. Moreover, my
dear sir, our little domestic difficulties must
not be suffered to interfere with the duties
of hospitality. It is high time that you
should have your supper; and I even venture
to ask that you will hurry your meal a little—
to the end that you may have opportunity,
before the departure of your train this evening, to see something of the brighter side of
our little town. After this sombre scene,
you will find, I trust, agreeable mental refreshment in witnessing—perhaps even in
participating in—our friendly card-playing,

and in taking part with us in our usual cheerful evening dance. By your leave, Brother
Wood, I will seat myself on the rear of your
buck-board and drive along with you into
town."

The little man was too jolted to say anything—and up Charley hiked on the back of
the buck-board, and away they went down
the road. The rest followed on after: with
the Hen holding fast to Kerosene, and Kerosene yelling for all she was worth; and behind
come some of the boys toting Blister's corpse
—with Blister swearing at 'em for the way
they had his legs twisted, and ending by kicking loose and making a break by the short-
cut back of the freight-house for home. The
other corpse — seeing the way Blister was
monkeyed with — stood off the ones that
wanted to carry him, allowing he'd be more
comfortable if he walked.

When the buck-board got down to the
deepo the little man said he felt sickish—not
being used to such goings-on — and didn't
care much for eating his supper; and he

Shorty Smith's Hanging

said he thought likely he'd be better if he
had a brandy-and-soda to settle his insides.
So him and Santa Fé went across to the
Forest Queen to get it—and the first thing
they struck was Blister, come to life again,
behind the bar!

Santa Fé hadn't counted on that card
coming out—but he shook one to meet it
down his sleeve, and played it as quick as
he knowed how. "Ah, Patrick," says he,
"so you have taken your poor brother's
place." And to the little man, who was
staring at Blister like a stuck pig, he says:
"They were twin brothers, sir, this gentleman and the deceased—and, as you see, so
alike that few of their closest friends could
tell them apart."

"It was worse than that," says Blister,
following right along with the same suit.
"Only when ŏne of us was drunk and the
other sober, and that way there being a difference betwane us, could we tell our own
selves apart—and indade I'm half for thinking that maybe it's meself, and not poor
Mike, that's been killed by Nosey Green this

day. But whichever of us it is that's dead, it's a domn good job—if your Reverence will excuse me saying so—the other one of us has made of Nosey: bad luck to the heart and lights of him, that are cooking this blessed minute in the hottest corner of hell!"

"Tut! Tut! Brother Patrick," says Santa Fé, speaking friendly but serious. "You know how strongly I feel about profanity—even when, as in the present instance, justly aroused resentment lends to it a colorable excuse. And also, my dear brother, I beg you to temper with charity your views as to Brother Green's present whereabouts. It is sufficient for all purposes of human justice that he has passed away. And now, if you please, you will supply our visitor, here—whose nerves not unnaturally are shaken by the tragic events of the past hour—with the brandy-and-soda that I am satisfied he really needs. In that need, my own nerves being badly disordered, I myself share; and as the agonizing loss that you have suffered has put a still more severe strain upon your nerves,

Shorty Smith's Hanging

Brother Patrick, I beg that you will join us. The drinks are on me."

"Sure your Reverence has a kind heart in you, and that's the holy truth," says Blister. "It's to me poor dead brother's health I'll be drinking, and with all the good-will in the world!"

They had another after that; and then Blister said there was luck in odd numbers, and he wanted to show Palomitas knowed how to be hospitable to strangers, and they must have one on the bar. They had it all right, and by that time—having the three of 'em in him—the little man said he was feeling better; but, even with his drinks to help him, when he come to eating his supper he didn't make out much of a meal. He seemed to be all sort of dreamy, and was like he didn't know where he was.

Santa Fé kept a-talking away to him cheerful while they was hashing; and when they'd finished off he told him he hoped what he'd see of the bright side of Palomitas—before his train started—would make him forget the cruelly sorrowful shadows of that melancholy

afternoon. He was a daisy at word-sling-
ing, Charley was—better'n most auctioneers.
Then they come along together back to the
bar-room—where the cloth was off the table,
and the cards and chips out, ready for business to begin. All the boys was jammed in
there—Nosey Green with his face tied up like
he had a toothache, so it didn't show who he
was—waiting to see what more was coming;
and they was about busting with the laughs
they had inside 'em, and ready to play close
up to Santa Fé's hand.

Charley set down to deal, same as usual,
and asked the little man to set down aside of
him—telling him he'd likely be interested in
knowing that what come to the bank that
night would go to getting the melodeon the
Sunday-school needed bad. And then he
shoved the cards round the table, and things
begun. The little man took it all dreamy—
saying kind of to himself he'd never in all
his born days expected to see a minister making money for Sunday-school melodeons by
running a faro-bank. But he wasn't so
dreamy but he had sense enough to keep out

Shorty Smith's Hanging

of the game. Santa Fé kept a-asking him polite to come in; but he kept answering back polite he wouldn't—saying he was no sort of a hand at cards.

About the size of it was, in all the matters he could see his way to that little man had as good a load of sand as anybody—and more'n most. Like enough at home he'd read a lot of them fool Wild West stories— the kind young fellers from the East, who swallow all that's told 'em, write up in books with scare pictures—and that was why in some ways he was so easy fooled. But I guess it would a-been a mistake to pick him up for a fool all round. Anyhow, Santa Fé got a set-back from him on his melodeon-faro racket—and set-backs didn't often come Santa Fé's way.

It wasn't a real game the little man was up against, and like enough he had the savey to ketch on to what was being give him. For the look of the thing they'd fixed to start with a baby limit, and not raise it till he got warmed up and asked to; and it was fixed only what he dropped—the rest going back

to the boys—should stay with the bank.
But as he didn't warm up any worth speaking of, and wasn't giving himself no chances
at all to do any dropping, Santa Fé pretty
soon found out they might as well hang up
the melodeon fund and go on to the next
turn.

The Sage - Brush Hen managed most of
what come next, and she done it well. She'd
dressed herself up in them white clothes of
hers with a little blue bow tied on at the
neck—looking that quiet and tidy and real
lady-like you'd never a-notioned what a
mixed lot she was truly—and she'd helped
the other girls rig out as near the same way
as they could come. Some of 'em didn't
come far; but they all done as well as they
knowed how to, and so they wasn't to be
blamed. Old Tenderfoot Sal—she was the
limit, Sal was—wasn't to be managed no
way; so they just kept her out of the show.
When Santa Fé come to see faro-banking
for melodeons wasn't money - making, he
passed out word to the Hen to start up her

Shorty Smith's Hanging

part of the circus—and in the Hen come, looking real pretty in her white frock, and put her hand on his shoulder married-like and says: "Now, my dear, it isn't fair for you gentlemen to keep us ladies waiting another minute longer. We want our share in the evening's amusement. Do put the cards away and let us have our dance." And then she says to the little man, nice and friendly: "My husband is so eager to get our melodeon—and we really do need it badly, of course—that I have trouble with him every night to make him stop the game and give us ladies the dance that we do so enjoy." And then she says on to Charley again: "How has the melodeon fund come out to-night, my dear?"

"Very well indeed. Very well indeed, my angel," Charley says back to her. "Eleven dollars and a half have been added to that sacred deposit; and the contributions have been so equally distributed that no one of us will feel the trifling loss. But in interrupting our game, my dear, you are quite right—as you always are. Our guest is not taking

part in it; and—as he cannot be expected
to feel, as we do, a pleasurable excitement
in the augmentation of our cherished little
hoard—we owe it to him to pass to a form
of harmless diversion in which he can have a
share." And then he says to the little man:
"I am sure, sir, that Mrs. Charles will be
charmed to have you for her partner in the
opening dance of what we playfully term
our ball."

"The pleasure will be mine," says the
little man—he was a real friendly polite little
old feller—and up he gets and bows to the
Hen handsome and gives her his arm: and
then in he went with her to the dance-hall,
with Santa Fé and the rest of us following
on. It give us a first-class jolt to find all
the girls so quiet-looking; and they being
that way braced up the whole crowd to be
like a dancing-party back East. To see the
boys a-bowing away to their partners, while
José—he was the fiddler, José was—was a
tuning up, you wouldn't a-knowed where
you was!

It was a square dance to start in with:

Shorty Smith's Hanging

with the little man and the Hen, and Charley
and Kerosene Kate, a-facing each other; and
Denver Jones with Carrots—that was the
only name she ever had in Palomitas—and
Shorty Smith and Juanita, at the sides.
Them three was the girls the Hen had done
best with; and she'd fixed 'em off so well
they most might have passed for back-East
school-ma'ams—at least, in a thickish crowd.
Everybody else just stood around and looked
on—and that time, with all the Forest Queen
ways of managing dancing upset, it was the
turn of the Palomitas folks to think they'd
struck a dream! The little man, of course,
didn't know he'd struck anything but what
went on always — and the way he kicked
around spirited on them short little fat legs
of his was just a sight to see!

Like as not he hadn't got a good sight of
Kerosene Kate while she was doing her killed
husband act before supper; or, maybe, it
was her being dressed up so tidy made a
difference. Anyways, he didn't at first
ketch on to her being about the freshest-
made widow he'd ever tumbled to in a

dancing-party. But he got there all right when the square dance was over, and José flourished his fiddle and sung out for the Señores and Señoritas to take partners for a *valsa*, and the Hen brought up Kerosene to foot it with him—telling him she was the organist who was going to play the melodeon when they got it, and he'd find her a nice partner as she was about the best dancer they had.

When he did size her up he was that took aback he couldn't talk straight. "But—but," says he, "isn't this the lady whose husband was—was—" and he stuck fast.

"Whose husband met with an accident this afternoon," says the Hen, helping him out with it. "Yes, this is our poor sister Rebecca—but the accident happened, you know, so many hours ago that the pang of it has passed; and—as Mr. Green, the gentleman who shot her husband, was shot right off himself—she feels, as we all do, that the incident is closed."

And then Kerosene put in: "Great Scott, mister, you don't know Palomitas! Widows

Shorty Smith's Hanging

in these parts don't set round moping their
heads off all the rest of their lives. They
wait long enough for politeness—same as I've
done—and then they start in on a new
deal."

The little man likely was too mixed up to
notice Kerosene didn't talk pretty, like Santa
Fé and the Hen knowed how to; and he was
so all-round jolted that before he knew it—
Kerosene getting a-hold of his hand with one
of hers, and putting the other on his shoulder
—he had his arm round her waist kind of by
instinct and was footing it away with her the
best he knowed how. But while he was a-
circling about with her he was the dreamiest
looking one you ever seen. Kerosene said
afterwards she heard him saying to himself
over and over: "This can't be real! This
can't be real!"

What happened along right away after
was real enough for him—at least, he thought
it was, and that come to the same thing. He
was so dizzied up when Kerosene stopped
dancing him—she was doing the most of it,
she said, he keeping his little fat legs going

'cause she swung him round and he had to—
all he wanted was to be let to set down. So
Kerosene set him—and then the next act
was put through.

Bill Hart and Shorty Smith come up to
Kerosene right together, and both of 'em
asked her polite if she'd dance. She said
polite she'd be happy to; but she said, seeing
both gentlemen had spoke at once for her,
they must fix it between 'em which one had
the call. All the same, she put her hand on
Hart's arm, like as if he was the one she
wanted—and of course that pleased Hart
and made Shorty mad. Then the two of 'em
begun talking to each other, Hart speaking
sarcastic and Shorty real ugly, and so things
went on getting hotter and hotter—till Kerosene, doing it like she meant to break up the
rumpus, shoved Hart's arm round her and
started to swing away. Just as they got
agoing, Shorty out with his gun and loosed
off at Hart with it—and down Hart went
in a heap on the floor.

The whole place, of course, right away
broke into yells and cusses, and everybody

"AND DOWN HART WENT IN A HEAP ON THE FLOOR"

Shorty Smith's Hanging

come a-crowding into a heap—some of the
boys picking up Hart and carrying him, kicking feeble real natural, out into the kitchen;
and some more grabbing a-hold of Shorty and
taking away his gun. Kerosene let off howls
fit to blow the roof off—only quieting down
long enough to say she'd just agreed to take
Hart for her second, and it was hard luck to
be made a widow of twice in one day. Then
she howled more. Really, things did go
with a hum!

Santa Fé and the rest come a-trooping
back from the kitchen — leaving the door
just a crack open, so Hart could peep through
and see the fun—and Santa Fé jumped up
on a bench and sung out "Order!" as loud
as he could yell. Knowing what was expected of 'em, the boys quieted down sudden; and the Hen got a-hold of Kerosene
and snuggled her up to her, and told her to
weep on her fond breast—and Kerosene
started in weeping on the Hen's fond breast
all right, and left off her howls. The room
was that quiet you could a-heard a cat purr.

"My brethren," says Charley, talking sad-

sounding and digging away at his eyes with
his pocket-handkerchief, "Brother Hart has
left us"—Hart being in the kitchen that was
dead true—"and for the third time to-day
our Sunshine Club has suffered a fatal loss.
Still more lamentable is the case of our
doubly stricken sister Rebecca — only just
recovered, by time's healing touch, from the
despair of her tragic widowhood, and at the
threshold of a new glad life of wedded happiness—who again is desolately bereaved."
(Kerosene give a dreadful groan—seeming to
feel something was expected of her—and
then jammed back to the Hen's fond breast
again and kept on a-weeping like a pump.)
"Our hearts are with Sister Rebecca in her
woe," says Charley. "She has all our sympathy, and the full help of our sustaining
love."

"If I know anything about the sense of
this meeting," Hill chipped in, "it's going to
do a damn sight more'n sling around sympathy." (Hill had a way of speaking careless, but he didn't mean no harm by it.)
"That shooting wasn't a square one," says

Shorty Smith's Hanging

Hill; "and it's likely there'll be another member missing from the Sunshine Club for doing it. There's telegraph-poles," says Hill, "right across the way!"

"Brother Hill is right," Santa Fé went on, "though I am pained that his unhappy disposition to profanity remains uncurbed. The shot that has laid low Brother Hart was a foul one. Justice, my friends, exemplary justice, must be meted out to the one who laid and lowered him; and I reckon the quicker we get Brother Smith over to the deepo, and up on the usual telegraph-pole—as Brother Hill has suggested—the better it 'll be for the moral record of our town. All in favor of such action will please signify it by saying 'Ay.'" And the whole crowd—except Shorty, who voted against it—yelled out "Ay" so loud it shook all the bottles in the bar.

"The ayes have it," says Santa Fé, "and we will proceed. Brother Wood, as chairman of the Friendly Aid Society, I beg that you will go on ahead to the deepo and get ready the rope that on these occasions you

so obligingly lend us from the Company's
stores. Brother Jones and Brother Hill,
you will kindly bring along the prisoner.
The remaining Friendly Aiders present will
have the goodness, at the appropriate moment, to render the assistance that they
usually supply." And off Charley went,
right after Wood, with the rest of us following on: Hill and Denver yanking along
Shorty and flourishing their guns savage;
the girls in a pack around the Hen holding
on to Kerosene; and Kerosene doing her
share of what was wanted by letting out
yells.

The little man was left to himself a-purpose; and he was so shook up, while he was
coming along with the crowd over to the
deepo, he couldn't say a word. But he
managed to get his stamps going, though
they didn't work well, when we was all on
the platform—waiting while Wood rigged
up the rope on the telegraph-pole—and he
asked Santa Fé, speaking husky, what the
boys meant to do.

"Justice!" says Charley, talking as digni-

Shorty Smith's Hanging

fied as a just-swore-in sheriff. "As I ex-
plained to you this morning, sir, nobody in
Palomitas ever stands in the way of a fair
fight—like the one you happened to come
in on at the finish a few hours ago—any more
than good citizens, elsewhere and under different conditions, interfere with the processes
of the courts. But when the fight is not fair,
as in the present instance—the gravamen of
the charge against Brother Smith being that
he loosed off into Brother Hart's back when
the latter did not know it was coming and
hadn't his gun out—then the moral sense of
our community crystallizes promptly into
the punitive action that the case demands:
as you will see for yourself, inside of the next
ten minutes, when you see Brother Smith
run up on that second telegraph-pole to the
left and kicking his legs in the air until he
kicks himself into Kingdom Come!"

"Good Heavens!" says the little man.
"You're not going to—to hang him?"

"We just rather are!" says Santa Fé.
And then he says, talking kind of cutting:
"May I ask, sir, what you do in England with

murderers? Do you pay 'em salaries, and ask 'em out to tea-parties, and hire somebody to see they have all the drinks they want?''

The little man begun telling how English folks manage such matters, and was real excited. But nobody but the Hen paid no attention to him. The Hen—she and Kerosene was standing close aside of him—turned round to him and said pleasant she always enjoyed most the hangings they had by moonlight (the moon was at the full, and shining beautiful) because the moonlight, she said, cast over them such a glamour of romance. And her looking at moonlight hangings that way seemed to give him such a jolt he stopped talking and give a kind of a gasp. There wasn't no more time for talking, anyway—for just then the train backed in to the platform and the conductor sung out the Friendly Aiders had got to get a move on 'em, if them going by it was to see the doings, and put Shorty through.

Being moonlight, and the shadows thick, helped considerable—keeping from showing how the boys had fixed Shorty up so his

Shorty Smith's Hanging

hanging wouldn't come hard: with a lariat
run round under his arms, his shirt over it,
and a loop just inside his collar where they
could hitch the rope fast. When they did
hitch to it, things looked just as natural as
you please.

Shorty got right into the hanging spirit—
he always was a comical little cuss, Shorty
was—pleading pitiful with the boys to let
up on him; and, when they wouldn't, getting a halt on 'em—same as he'd seen done
at real hangings—by beginning to send messages to all the folks he ever had. Santa Fé
let him go on till he'd got to his uncles and
cousins—and then he said he guessed the
rest of the family could make out to do with
second-hand messages from them that had
them; and as it was past train-time, and the
distinguished stranger in their midst—who
was going on it—would enjoy seeing the show
through, the hanging had got to be shoved
right along. When Charley'd give his order,
Carver come up—he was the Pullman conductor, Carver was, and he had his points
how to manage—and steered the little man

onto the back platform of the Pullman,
where he could see well; and so had things
all ready for the train to pull out as soon as
Shorty was swung off.

Wood, who'd had experience, had the rope
rigged up in good shape over the cross-bar
of the telegraph-pole; and Hill and Denver
fetched old Shorty along—with Shorty letting
on he was scared stiff, and yowling like he'd
been ashamed to if it hadn't been a bunco
game he was playing—and hitched him to
it, with the boys standing close round in a
clump so they hid the way it was done.

The little man was so worked up by that
time—it likely being he hadn't seen much of
hangings—he was just a-hopping: with his
plug hat off, and sousing the sweat off his
face with his pocket-handkerchief, and singing out what was going on wasn't any better
than murder, and begging all hands not to
do what he said was such a dreadful deed.

But nobody paid no attention to him
(except Carver, he was a friendly feller, Carver was, kept a lookout he didn't tumble
himself off the platform) and when Denver

Shorty Smith's Hanging

sung out things was ready, and Santa Fé
sung out back for the Friendly Aiders to haul
away, the boys all grabbed onto the rope
together—and up Shorty went a-kicking into
the air.

Shorty really did do his act wonderful:
kicking every which way at first, and then
only sort of squirming, and then quieting
down gradual till he just hung limp—with
the kick all kicked out of him—turning
round and round slow!

When he'd quieted, the train conductor
swung his lantern to start her, and off she
went—the little man standing there on the
back platform of the Pullman, a-grabbing
at the railing like he was dizzy, looking back
with all his eyes.   And old Shorty up on the
telegraph-pole, making a black splotch twisting about in the moonlight, was the last bit
of Palomitas he seen!

Next day but one Carver come down again
on his regular run, and he told the boys the
little man kept a-hanging onto the platform
railing and a-looking back hard till the train

got clean round the curve. Then he give a kind of a coughing groan, Carver said, and come inside the Pullman—there wasn't no other passengers that night in the Pullman—and plumped himself down on a seat anyways, a-looking as white as a clean paper collar; and for a while he just set there, like he had a pain.

At last he roused up and reached for his grip and got his flask out and had a good one; and when he'd had it he says to Carver, as savage as if Carver—who hadn't had no hand in the doings—was the whole business: "Sir, this America of yours is a continent of chaos — and you Americans are no better than so many wild beasts!" Then he had another; and after that he went on, like he was talking to himself: "All I ask is to get out of this nightmare of a country in a hurry —and safe back to my own home in the Avenue Road!" And from then on, Carver said, till it was bedtime—except now and then he took another—he just set still and glared.

Carver said it wasn't any funeral of his,

Shorty Smith's Hanging

and so he didn't see no need to argue with
him.   And he allowed, he said, maybe he
had some call to feel the way he did about
America, and to want to get quick out of it,
after being up against Palomitas for what
he guessed you might say was a full day.

VII

THE PURIFICATION OF PALOMITAS

IN the long run, same as I said to start with, all tough towns gets to where it's needed to have a clean-up. Shooting-scrapes is a habit that grows; and after a while decent folks begins to be sort of sick of such doings—and of having things all upside-downey generally—and then something a little extry happens, bringing matters to a head, and the white men take hold and the toughs is fired. Just to draw a card anywheres from the pack—there was Durango. What made a clean town of Durango was that woman getting killed in bed in her tent—the boys being rumpussing around, same as usual, and a shot just happening her way and taking her. It was felt

The Purification of Palomitas

that outsiders—and 'specially ladies—oughtn't
to get no such treatment; and so they had a
spring house-cleaning—after what I reckon
was the worst winter a town ever went
through—and Durango was sobered right
down.

Palomitas went along the same trail, and
took the same pass over the divide. All
through that year, while the end of the track
hung there, things kept getting more and
more uncomfortabler. When construction
started up again—the little Englishman, in
spite of the dose we give him, reported favor-
able on construction and the English stockholders put up the stake they was asked to—
things got to be worse still. Right away, as
soon as work begun, the place was jammed
full of Greasers getting paid off every Saturday night, and all day Sunday being crazy
drunk and knifing each other, and in between
scrappings having their pay sucked out of
'em at the banks and dance-halls—and most
of the boys going along about the same rate,
except they used guns instead of knives to
settle matters—so the town really was just

about what you might call a quarter-section of hell's front yard.

Being that way, it come to be seen there'd got to be a clean-up; and what was wanted for a starter was give by Santa Fé Charley shooting Bill Hart. There was no real use for the shooting. The two of 'em just got to jawing in Hart's store about which was the best of two brands of plug tobacco—Hart being behind the counter, and Charley, who had a bad jag on, setting out in the middle of the store on a nail-kag—and the first thing anybody knowed, Charley'd let go with his derringer through his pants-pocket and Hart was done for. If Santa Fé hadn't been on one of his tears at the time, the thing wouldn't a-happened—him and Hart always having been friendly, and 'specially so after the trouble they'd had together over Hart's aunt. But when it did happen—being so sort of needless, and Hart popular—most of us made our minds up something had got to be done.

Joe Cherry headed the reform movement.

The Purification of Palomitas

He had a bunch of sheep up in the Sangre de Cristo mountains, Cherry had, but was in town frequent and always bunked at Hart's store—him and Hart having knowed each other back East and being great friends. That made him take a 'special interest in the matter; and when he come a-riding in about an hour after things was over—likely he'd a-fixed Santa Fé himself if he'd been there when it happened—he got right up on his ear. He said he meant to square accounts for Bill's shooting, and he reckoned telegraph-poling Charley was about what was needed to square 'em; and he said it was a good time, with that for a starter, for rounding-up and firing all the toughs there was in town. The rest of us allowed Cherry's notions was reasonable, and it was seen there'd better be no fooling over 'em; and so we went straight on and had a meeting, with Cherry chairman, and fixed up a Committee—and the Committee begun business by corralling Santa Fé, and then set to work and made out a list of them that was to be fired.

There was about a dozen of 'em in the list;

and they was told—the notice being posted
at the deepo—they had twenty-four hours to
get out in; and it was added that them that
wasn't out in twenty-four hours would find
'emselves landed on the dumps for keeps. A
few of 'em kicked a little—saying it was a free
country, and they guessed they'd a right to
be where they'd a mind to. But when the
Committee said back it just was a free country, and one of the freest things in it was
telegraph-poles—as Santa Fé Charley was
going to find out for certain, and as them that
was ordered to get up and get and didn't
would find out along with him—even the
kickingest of 'em seen they'd better just shut
their heads and andy along.

It wasn't till the Committee come to tackle
the Sage-Brush Hen there was any trouble—
and then they found their drills was against
quartz! Two or three of Charley's worst
shootings was charged to the Hen, she being
'special friends with him; and just because she
was such a good-natured obliging sort of a
woman, always wanting to please everybody,
she was at the roots of half the fights that

The Purification of Palomitas

started in—so there'd come to be what was called the Hen's Lot out in the cemetery on the mesa, as I've mentioned before. The Committee put her in their list because they knowed for a fact there was bound to be ructions in Palomitas as long as she stayed there; and so they found 'emselves in a deepish hole when she said plump Palomitas suited her, and she didn't mean to be fired. The Hen knowed as well as they did she had a cinch on 'em. If they didn't like her staying, she said, they could yank her up to the next telegraph-pole to Charley's—and then she asked 'em, kind of cool and cutting, if they didn't think hanging a lady would give a nice name to the town!

The Committee was in session in the waiting-room at the deepo while the Hen was doing her talking, and Santa Fé—with handcuffs on, and tied to the express messenger's safe—was in the express office, with the door open between. Everybody seen the Hen was right, and hanging her would be ungentlemanly, and nobody seemed to know what they'd better do. While they was all

setting still and thinking, Santa Fé spoke up
from the express office—saying he had the
reputation of the town at heart as much as
anybody, and to make a real clean-up the
Hen ought to quit along with the others,
and if they'd let him have five minutes
private talk with her he'd fix things so she'd
go.

The Committee didn't much believe Santa
Fé could deliver the goods; but they seen it
would be a way out for 'em if he did—and so
they agreed him and the Hen should have
their talk. To make it private, he was took
out and hitched fast to a freight-car laying on
the siding back of the deepo—the Committee
standing around in easy shooting distance,
but far enough off not to hear nothing, with
their Winchesters handy in case the Hen took
it into her head to cut the rope and give him
a chance to get away. She didn't—and she
and Santa Fé talked to each other mighty
serious for a while; and then they begun to
snicker a little; and they ended up in a
rousing laugh.

Charley sung out they'd finished, and the

The Purification of Palomitas

Committee closed in and unhitched him, and took him back to the express office and hitched him to the safe again—where he was to stay till hanging-time, with members of the Committee taking turns keeping him quiet with their guns. He said he was much obliged to 'em, and the Hen had agreed to quit—and everybody was pleased all round.

"I don't like not being here when Charley gets his medicine," the Hen said, "him and me being such good friends; but he says it would only worry him having me in the audience, and so I've promised him I'll light out"—and she kept her word, and got away for Denver by that night's train. Her going took a real load off the Committee's mind.

Some of the other fired ones went off on the same train. The rest took Hill's coach across to Santa Fé—and made no trouble, Hill said, except they held the coach for two hours at Pojuaque while all hands got drunk at old man Bouquet's. Hill said all the rest of the way they was yelling, and firing off their guns, and raising hell generally—that was the way Hill put it—but they didn't do no real harm.

Santa Fé's Partner

It was Joe Cherry's notion that Santa Fé should be took along to Hart's funeral, and not hung till everybody got back to town again. Joe was a serious-minded man, and he said the moral effect of running things that way would pan out a lot richer than if they just had a plain hanging before the funeral got under way.

Santa Fé kicked at that, at first; and a good many of the boys felt he had a right to. Santa Fé said it was all in the game to run him up to the telegraph-pole in front of the deepo, the same as other folks; but no committee had no right, he said, to make a circus of him by packing him all round the place after poor old Bill—who always had been plain in his tastes, and would have been the last man in Palomitas to want that kind of a fuss made over him—and he didn't mean to take a hand in no such fool carryings-on. He didn't want anybody to think he was squirming, he said, for he wasn't. Some men got up against telegraph-poles, and others got up against guns or pneumonia or whatever happened to come along—and it was all

The Purification of Palomitas

in the day's work. But when they did get
up against it—whatever it turned out to be
—that was the one time in their lives when it
wasn't fair to worry 'em more'n was needed.
Nobody but chumps, he said, would want to
hurt his feelings by making him do trick-mule
acts at poor old Bill's funeral—'specially as
him and Bill always had been friendly, and
nobody was sorrier than he was about the
accident that had occurred.

Santa Fé was a first-rate talker, and everybody but Cherry allowed what he was letting
out had a good deal of sense in it. He ended
up by saying that if they did make any such
fool show of him he'd like 'em to put it
through quick and get him back to the deepo
and telegraph him off to Kingdom Come in a
hurry—as he'd be glad at any price to be shut
of a crowd that would play it on anybody
that low down!

Cherry stuck it out, though, to have things
his way. Palomitas was going in for purification, Cherry said, and the moral effect of
having Santa Fé along at Bill's funeral was
part of the purifying. The very fact that

Santa Fé's Partner

Santa Fé was kicking so hard against it, he said, showed it was a good thing. There was sense in that, too; and so the upshot of it was the boys come round to Cherry's plan. The only serious thing against it was it meant waiting over another day, till the funeral outfit got down from Denver—all hands having chipped in to give Hart a good send-off, and telegraphed his size to a first-class Denver undertaker, with orders to do him up in style. Making him wait around so long, sort of idle, was what Santa Fé kicked hardest against at first. But after his talk with the Hen, as was remembered afterwards, he didn't do any more kicking; and some of the boys noticed he was a little nervous, and kept asking, off and on, if they still meant to run the show that way.

The boys did what they could to make the time go for him—setting around sociable in the express office telling stories about other hangings they'd happened to get up against, and trying all they knowed how to amuse him, and giving him more seegars and drinks than he really cared to have. But as he

The Purification of Palomitas

was kept hitched to both handles of the safe right enough, and handcuffed, and as the two members of the Committee watching him—while they was as pleasant with him as anybody—never had their hands far off their guns, it's likely there'd been other times when he'd enjoyed himself more.

Things was spirited at the deepo when the Denver train got in. All there was of Palomitas was on deck, and Becker'd come over from Santa Cruz de la Cañada, and old man Bouquet from Pojuaque, and Sam and Marcus Elbogen had driven across on their buck-board from San Juan—and Mexicans had come in from all around in droves.

The Elbogen brothers had been asked over for the funeral 'special—because they both had good voices, and the Committee thought like enough, being Germans, they'd know some hymns. It turned out they didn't—but they blew off " The Watch on the Rhine " in good shape, when singing time come out at the cemetery; and as it was a serious-sounding tune it done just as well. Singing it made

trouble, though: because Hart's nephew—
who knowed German and was a pill—hadn't
no more sense'n to tell old man Bouquet,
coming back to town, what the words meant;
and that started old man Bouquet off so—
the war not being long over, and his side
downed—that it took two of us, holding him
by his arms and legs, to keep him from trying to fight both the Elbogens at once.
Being good-natured young fellows, the Elbogens didn't take offence, but behaved like
perfect gentlemen—telling old man Bouquet
they didn't mean to hurt his feelings, and
was sorry if they had—and it ended up well
by their having drinks together at the Forest
Queen. All that, though, has no real bearing
on the story. It happened along later in the
day.

Before the train got in, to save time, a rope
had been rigged for Santa Fé over the cross-
bar of the usual telegraph-pole—and Cherry,
who knowed how to manage better'n most,
had seen to it the rope was well soaped so as
to run smooth. Cherry said he'd knowed
things go real annoying, sometimes, when the

The Purification of Palomitas

soap had been forgot. Santa Fé looked well.
He'd had a good brush up—and he needed it,
after being tied fast to the safe for three days
and sleeping in a blanket on the express-
office floor—and he'd put on a clean shirt,
and blacked his boots, and had a shave. He
always was a tidy sort of a man.

When the train pulled in, being on time for
a wonder, some fellows from Chamita and
the Embudo—come to see the doings—got
out from the day-coach and shook hands; and
the Denver undertaker got out from the express-car and helped the messenger unload
the fixings he'd brought for poor old Bill.
Everybody stood around quiet like, and as
serious as you please. You might have
thought it was a Sunday morning back in the
States.

Except now and then a drummer—bound
for Santa Fé on Hill's coach—nobody much
ever come to Palomitas on the Pullman;
and so there was something of a stir-up when
the Pullman conductor helped a lady out of
the car—landing her close to where Charley
in his clean shirt and handcuffs on was stand-

ing between two members of the Committee holding guns. She was a fine-shaped woman, but looked oldish—as well as you could see for the veil she had on—having a sad pale face a good deal wrinkled and a bunch of gray hair. She was dressed in measly old black clothes, and had an old black shawl on, and looked poor.

Getting out into that crowd of men seemed to rattle her, and she didn't for a minute look at nobody. It wasn't till she a'most butted into Charley she seen him—and when she did see him she let off a yell loud enough to give points to a locomotive! And then she sort of sobbed out: "My husband!"—and got her arms around Santa Fé's neck and begun to cry.

"My God! It's my wife!" said Charley. And if the members of the Committee hadn't caught the two of 'em quick they'd likely tumbled down.

Santa Fé was the first to get his wind back. "My poor darling!" he said. "To think that you should have come to me at last—and in this awful hour!"

The Purification of Palomitas

"What does it mean, Charley? Tell me, what does it mean?" she moaned.

Santa Fé snuggled her up to him—as well as he could with his hands handcuffed—and said back to her: "It means, Mary, that in less than two hours' time I am to be hung! In the heat of passion I have killed a man. It was more than half an accident, as everybody here knows"—and he looked over her head at the boys as they all jammed in to listen—"but that don't matter, so far as the dreadful result is concerned. I loved the man I shot like my own brother, and shooting him in that chance way has about broken my heart. But that don't count either. Justice must be done, my darling. Stern justice must be done. You have come just in time to see your husband die!" He was quiet for a minute, with the woman all in a shake against him—and a kind of a snuffling went through the crowd. Then he said, sort of choky: "Tell me, Mary, how are our dear little girls?"

She was too broke up to answer him. She just kept on hugging him, and crying as hard as she could cry.

Santa Fé's Partner .

"Gentlemen," said Santa Fé, "it is better that this painful scene should end. Take my poor wife from me, and let me pay the just penalty of my accidental crime. Take her away, please—and hang me as quick as you can!"

"They sha'n't hang you, Charley! They sha'n't! They sha'n't!" she sung out—and she jerked away from him and got in front of Cherry and pitched down on the deepo platform on her knees. "Don't hang him, sir!" she groaned out. "Spare him to me, and to our dear little girls who love him with all their little hearts! Oh, sir, say that he shall be saved!"

"Get up, ma'am, please," Cherry said, looking as worried as he could look. "That's no sort of a way for a lady to do! Please get up right away."

"Never! Never!" she said. "Never till you promise me that the life of my dear husband shall be spared!"—and she grabbed Cherry round the knees and groaned dreadful. He really was the most awkward-looking man, with her holding onto his legs that way, you ever seen!

"'DON'T HANG HIM, SIR!' SHE GROANED OUT"

The Purification of Palomitas

"Oh, Lord, ma'am, *do* get up!" he said. "Having you like that for another minute 'll make me sick. I'm not used to such goings-on"—and Cherry did what he could to work loose his legs.

But she hung on so tight he couldn't shake her, and kept saying, "Save him! Save him!" and uttering groans.

Cherry wriggled his legs as much as he could and looked around at the boys. They all was badly broke up, and anybody could see they was weakening. "Shall we let up on Santa Fé this time?" he asked. "I guess it's true he didn't more'n half mean, being drunk the way he was, to shoot Bill—and it makes things different, anyway, knowing he's got kids and a wife. Bill himself would be the first to allow that. Bill was as kind-hearted a man as ever lived. Do please, ma'am, let go."

Nobody spoke for a minute—but it was plain how the tide was setting—and then Santa Fé himself chipped in. "Gentlemen," he said, "you all know I've faced this music from the first without any squirming, and even come into Joe Cherry's plan for making me do circus stunts at the funeral for the good of the town. I'm ready to go through the whole fool business right now, and come back here when it's all over and be hung according to contract—"

"Save him! Save him!" the woman sung out; and she give such a jerk to Cherry's legs it come close to spilling him.

"But I will say this much, gentlemen," Santa Fé went on: "I am willing to ask for the sake of my dear wife and helpless innocent infants what I wouldn't be low down enough to ask for myself—and that is that you call this game off. This dreadful experience has changed me, gentlemen. It has changed me right down to my toes. Being as close to a telegraph-pole as I am now makes a man want to turn over a new leaf and behave—as some of you like enough 'll find out for yourselves if you don't draw cards from my awful example and brace up all you know how. Give me another show, gentlemen. That's what I ask for—give me another show. Let me go home with my

The Purification of Palomitas

angel wife to the dear old farm in Ohio, where my aged mother and my sweet babes are waiting for me. Like enough they're standing out by the old well in the front yard looking down the road for me now!" Santa Fé gagged so he couldn't go on for a minutè. But he pulled himself together and finished with his chest out and his chin up and speaking firm. "Let me go home, I say, to the old farm and my dear ones—and take a fresh start at leading bravely the honest life of an honest man!"

Then he lowered down his chin and took his chest in and said, sort of soft and gentle: "Let go of Mr. Cherry's legs and come and kiss me, my darling! And please wipe the tears from my eyes—with my poor shackled hands I can't!"

The woman give Cherry's legs one more rousing jerk, and said, sort of imploring: "Save him! Save him for his old mother's sake, and for mine, and for the sake of our little girls!" Then she got up and wiped away at Santa Fé's eyes with her pocket-handkerchief, and went to kissing him for all she was worth—holding on to him tight around the neck with both arms.

The boys was all as uncomfortable as they could be—except Cherry seemed to feel better at getting his legs loose—and some of 'em fairly snuffled out loud. They stood around looking at each other, and nobody said a word. Then Santa Fé kind of wrenched loose from her kissing him and spoke up. "Which is it to be, gentlemen?" he said. "Is it the telegraph-pole—or is it another chance?" The woman moaned fit to break her heart.

The silence, except for her moaning, hung on for a good minute. Then Hill broke it. "Oh, damn it all!" said Hill—it was Hill's way to talk sort of careless—"Give him another chance!"

That settled things. In another minute they had the handcuffs off of Santa Fé and all the boys was shaking hands with him. And then they was asking to be introduced to his wife—she was all broke to bits, and crying, and kept her veil down—and shaking hands with her too; and they ended off by

The Purification of Palomitas

giving Charley and his wife three cheers.
You never seen folks so pleased! The only
one out of it was the Denver undertaker—
who couldn't be expected to feel like the
rest of us; and was in a hurry, anyway, to
put through his job so he could start back
home on the night train.

"You come along with me in the coach,
Charley," Hill said—Hill always was a friendly sort of a fellow—"and I'll jerk you over
to Santa Fé in no time, and you can start
right off East by the 6.30 train. That 'll be
quicker'n going up to Pueblo, and it 'll be
cheaper too. The ride across sha'n't cost
you a cent. If you and your lady come in
my coach, you come free. And I say, boys,"
Hill went on, "let's open a pot for them little
girls! Here's my hat, with ten dollars in it
for a warmer. I'd make it more if I could—
and nobody 'll hurt my feelings by raising my
call."

All hands made a rush for Hill's hat—and
when Hill handed it to that poor woman,
who had her pocket-handkerchief up to her
eyes under her veil and was crying so she

shook all over, there was more'n two hunderd dollars in it, mostly gold. "This is for
them children, ma'am, with all our compli-
ments," Hill said—and he and Charley helped
her hold her shawl up, so it made a kind of
a bag, while he turned his hat upside-down.

"Speaking for my dear little girls, I thank
you from my heart, gentlemen," Santa Fé
said. "This is a royal gift, and it comes at a
mighty good time. Some part of it must be
used to pay our way East—back to the dear
old home, where those little angels are waiting for us sitting cuddled up on their grand-
mother's knees. What remains, I promise
you gentlemen, shall be a sacred deposit—to
be used in buying little dresses, and hats, and
things, for my sweet babes. I hate to use a
single cent of it for anything else, but the
fact is just now I'm right down to the hard-
pan." And everybody—remembering Santa
Fé'd took advantage of being on his drunk
to get cleaned out at Denver Jones's place
the night before the shooting—knowed this
was true.

"Well, Charley, we must be andying along,"

The Purification of Palomitas

Hill said. "Waiting here to see you hung has put me more'n an hour behind on my schedule. I'll have to hustle them mules like hell"—that was the careless way Hill talked always—"if we're going to ketch that 6.30 train."

Everybody shook hands for good-bye with Santa Fé and his wife, and Santa Fé had his pockets stuffed full of seegars, and more bottles was put in the coach than was needed —and then we give 'em three cheers again, and away they went down the slope to the bridge over the Rio Grande, with Hill whipping away for all he was worth and cussing terrible at his mules. Whipping done some good, Hill used to say; but cuss-words was the only sure things to make mules go.

"Well, boys," said Cherry, when the yelling let up a little. "I guess getting shut of Santa Fé that way is better'n hanging him; and I guess—with him and the Hen and the rest of 'em fired out of it—we've got Palomitas purified about down to the ground. And what's to all our credits, we've ended off by doing a first-class good deed! Them little girls 'll be pleased and happy when their mother gets back to 'em with our money in her pocket, and brings along in good shape their father — who'd just about be in the thick of his kicking on that telegraph-pole, by this time, if she hadn't romped in the way she did on the closest kind of a close call!

"And now let's turn to and get poor old Bill planted. We've kind of lost sight of Bill in the excitement—and we owe him a good deal. If Santa Fé hadn't started the reform movement by shooting him, we'd still be going on in the same old way. You may say it's all Bill's doings that Palomitas has been give the clean-up it wanted, and wanted bad!"

When Hill drove into town next afternoon —coming to the deepo, where most of the boys was setting around waiting for the train to pull out—he was laughing so he was most tumbling off the box.

"I've got the damnedest biggest joke on this town," Hill said—Hill had the habit of

The Purification of Palomitas

talking that offhand way—"that ever was got on a town since towns begun!"

Hill was so full of it he couldn't hold in to make a story. He just went right on blurting it out: "Do you boys know who that wife of Charley's was that blew in yesterday from Denver? I guess you don't! Well, *I* do—she was the Sage-Brush Hen! Yes sirree," Hill said, so full of laugh he couldn't hardly talk plain; "that's just who she was! All along from the first there was something about her shape I felt I ought to know, and I was dead right. It come out while we was stopping at Bouquet's place at Pojuaque for dinner—they both knowing I'd see it was such a joke I wouldn't spoil it by giving it away too soon. She went in the back room at Bouquet's to have a wash and a brush up—and when she come along to table she'd got over being Charley's wife and was the Hen as good as you please! She hadn't a gray hair or a wrinkle left nowhere, and was like she always was except for her black clothes. When she saw my looks at seeing her, she got to laughing fit to kill herself—

just the same gay old Hen as ever; and she
always was, you know, the most comical-
acting sort of a woman, when she wanted
to be, anybody ever seen.

"When she quieted down her laughing a
little she told me the whole story. She and
Charley'd fixed it up between 'em, she said;
and she'd whipped up to Denver on one train
and down again on the next—buying quick
her gray hair and her black outfit, and getting
somebody she knowed at the Denver theatre
to fix her face for her so she'd look all broke
up and old. She nearly gave the whole thing
away, she said, when Charley asked her about
the little girls. He just throwed that in, without her expecting it—and it set her to laughing and shaking so, back of her veil, that
we'd a-ketched up with her sure, she said,
if Charley hadn't whispered quick to pretend
to cry and carry off her laughing that way.
She had another close call, she said, when
Charley was talking about the old farm in
Ohio—she all the time knowing for a fact
he was born in East St. Louis, and hadn't
any better acquaintance with Ohio than three

234

months in the Cincinnati jail. Charley
ought to go on the stage, she says—where
she's been herself. She says he'd lay Forrest
and Booth and all them fellows out cold!

"She and Charley just yelled while she was
telling it all to me; and they was laughing
'emselves 'most sick all the rest of the way
across to Santa Fé. When we got into town
I drove 'em to the Fonda; and then the Hen
rigged herself out in good clothes she bought
at Morse's—it was the pot we made up for
them sweet babes paid for her outfit—and
give her old black duds to one of the Mexican
chambermaids. They allowed — knowing I
could be trusted not to go around talking in
Santa Fé—they'd stay on at the Fonda till
to-morrow, anyway: so I might let 'em know,
when I get back again, how you boys took it
when you was told how they'd played it on
you right smack down to the ground!

"Charley sent word he hoped there wouldn't
be no hard feeling—as there oughtn't to be,
he said, seeing he was so drunk when he shot
Bill it was just an accident not calling for
hanging; and the whole thing, anyways, being

235

all among friends. And the Hen sent word
she guessed the two of 'em had give you a
first - class theatre show worth more'n you
put in my hat for gate-money, and you all
ought to be pleased. And they both said
they'd been treated so square by you fellows
they'd be real sorry to have any misunderstanding, and they hoped you'd take the
joke friendly—the same as they meant it
themselves."

Well, of course we all did take it friendly—
it wouldn't a-been sensible to take as good a
joke as that was any other way. Cherry was
the only one that squirmed a little. "It's on
us, and it's on us good," Cherry said; "and
I'm not kicking—only you boys haven't got
no notion what it is having a woman a-
grabbing fast to your legs and groaning at
you, and how dead sick it makes you feel!"

Cherry stopped for a minute, and looked as
if he was a'most sick with just thinking about
it. Then he sort of shook himself and got a
brace on, and went ahead with his chin up
like he was making a speech in town-meeting

The Purification of Palomitas

—and it turned out, as it don't always in town-meeting speeches, what he said was true.

"Gentlemen," said Cherry, "there's this to be said, and we have a right to say it proudly: we've give this town the clean-up we set out to give it, and from now on it's going to stay clean. There won't be any more doings; or, if there is, the Committee 'll know the reason why. Palomitas is purified, gentlemen, right down to the roots; and I reckon I'm mistook bad—worse'n I was when the Hen was yanking my legs about— if the Committee hasn't sand enough and rope enough to keep on keeping it pure!"

THE END